CHÂTEAUNOIR

CHÂTEAUNOIR

Peter Harvey joins a privateer that is sailing from Plymouth to fight the French. War, however, is not what it seems and his ideals are shattered when his ship is sunk and he is thrown into irons. Escape from Châteaunoir amid the hatred and terror of the French Revolution, and a meeting with Mademoiselle Louise de Chauvelin bring Peter to the swift conclusion that the French have enough problems without fighting wars. Is Châteaunoir to claim more from Louise than her father and her fire ravaged home?

Châteaunoir

by

Patricia Hemstock

Dales Large Print Books
Long Preston, North Yorkshire,
England.

British Library Cataloguing in Publication Data.

Hemstock, Patricia
    Châteaunoir.

    A catalogue record for this book is
    available from the British Library

    ISBN 1-85389-703-5 pbk

First published in Great Britain by Robert Hale, 1978

Published in Large Print 1997 by arrangement with the
copyright holder.

Dales Large Print is an imprint of
Library Magna Books Ltd.
Printed and bound in Great Britain by
T.J. International Ltd., Cornwall, PL28 8RW.

ONE

A lady walked with surprising calmness up the rough, wooden steps. Her hair was white, yet she had not reached even middle-age, and on her short clipped curls she wore a simple bonnet. Some who watched that day would remember her so, but most would recapture the picture of the vivacious Austrian, whose beautiful but extravagant gowns had once been the talk of Paris and Versailles. A lady whose fingers, now clasped in penitent prayer, had glittered and shone with diamonds. The mob in the square began shouting: *'Antoinette à la lanterne'*. They chanted it over and over again, stopping only to break into song for a while. *'Allons enfants de la Patrie...'* strains of La Marseillaise rose and fell like an angry tide.

It was the sixteenth of October 1793; Marie Antoinette stepped with dignity to the guillotine, and the crowd were hushed for a moment before the shouts began again. *'Liberté!'* *'Egalité!'* *'Fraternité!'*

Her husband, Louis XVI of France had been executed in January of that same year. Their beloved France was in turmoil, struggling under the ruthless hands of the Jacobins, Robespierre and Danton. At war with the Austrians and the Prussians, she had, on February the first, declared war on England. Now, even English men-o-war sailed against her.

Across the channel this day, this bright sunny afternoon of autumn, Michael Pendeen slipped unnoticed from his low roofed, Cornish home. The coat he wore was of dark blue which contrasted handsomely with his fine white shirt and muslin cravat. His breeches were of good quality, black worsted; his boots black leather. Quickly, he crossed to the granite walled stables and threw a saddle on his horse.

The air was crisp as he rode away from the house; the scent of roses mingled with the fragrance of late honeysuckle. The tall chestnuts and sprawling oaks bore their autumn glory with the dignity which befitted their great age. The hedgerows glowed crimson above the stark brown of the hawthorn. Harvest time had come early, the corn ripened well, and the barns were full to the roof.

Michael left the copse and turned his grey into a narrow, winding lane; heading her westwards towards the Atlantic coast. Within minutes, he reined her in, sighed, and relaxed in the saddle, maintaining a steady trot; as ahead of him rose a cloud of thick, grey dust.

Peter Harvey had dismounted by the time his sister's husband caught up with him. His sorrel mare nosed the cliff top turf with interest. Peter himself stood quite still, staring out over the grey-blue sea, his hands placed firmly on his hips. The biting westerly had dropped for a while, resting itself before blowing up again to cut at the bare faces of any unfortunate traveller. The sea flipped white froth onto the granite below, retreating at once as if caught in some mischievous deed.

Peter turned swiftly, startled when he heard the approaching hoofbeats. 'Michael!' he exclaimed with surprise. 'Are you seeking me?'

Michael laughed, springing down from his grey. 'Aye, but not for ought wrong. I wanted to talk away from the house.'

Peter nodded, looking back over the

rolling Atlantic with a sigh. The time had come as he had known it would. He lifted his leather-booted foot onto the flat edge of a granite boulder, and elbow on knee, he leaned a young chin in cupped hand. His fair hair was taken back into a brown, velvet bow. Of the same rich brown colour was his coat and beneath it the brilliant yellow of his embroidered waistcoat. His slender figure cut a fine sight against the blue of the sky. Even bluer were his bright eyes, now thoughtful, now shadowed by his furrowed brow as he considered the future.

When he and his younger brother Ben had run away from their Nottinghamshire home all of three years before, they could never have foreseen the consequential change in their lives. They had considered it adventurous to travel to Cornwall and seek work with smugglers. When their sister Rosalie had left Charlesworth Hall, their elegant home, to find them, she had met Cornishman Michael Pendeen. A smuggler himself, he had been the only person willing to help her in her search for her brothers. That Rosalie, then a twenty year old, orphaned, self-determined young lady should have fallen in love with

Michael had perhaps been inevitable. But their love had been so beset by problems that even now, looking back, they seemed insurmountable. When Peter brought the news that Ben had been imprisoned in France, Michael had at once taken his own lugger to rescue him. That action, although successful in its task, had cost him his boat and his freedom on English soil. A revenue cutter had wrecked his craft which was carrying illicit cargo and he had needed to sign on as mate on an America-bound packet schooner to escape arrest. During the year that Michael was exiled to sea, Rosalie had, unknown to him, continued to run the smuggling ring which he had built up and eventually she had secured his pardon. When on his homecoming he returned to England, a free man, he and Rosalie had married and he had vowed his intention of working towards having boats which conveyed only legal cargo.

It was three months now since the last of Michael's boats had carried contraband. The ships, now four in number, either fished or conveyed legal merchandise to Ireland or the Mediterranean Coast. The purchase of the seine boats, the large vertical net and fish cellars for a pilchard business was a further sign of Michael's tenacity. Peter, ten years his junior, worked as his partner.

Michael dismounted now, freed his horse to grass and came towards Peter. For once, the black eyes which laughed so much were solemn. The black curled hair, once worn loose, was tied back like that of his companion. Fifteen months of joy, of marriage to Rosalie had filled the once too lean face, but tall as Peter was, Michael stood a good two inches higher.

'There's something amiss,' he stated bluntly. 'You've a temper not in keeping with your nature. Rosalie is worried!'

Peter looked back from the sea; up at the man who stood beside him. There was no man on earth he respected more, yet his recent thoughts gave no merit to that fact. 'You want me to speak plain?' he enquired, dropping his boot to the ground and straightening his back.

'Do I not speak so?' Michael reminded him, a faint flicker of amusement in his eyes.

Peter nodded. It was true enough, yet not always easy to do.

'I'm concerned about the war,' he said slowly, 'that we take no part in it. We've good ships, good loyal men yet we fish and carry cargo like...like cowards.' He wished at once he had not used that word.

'You'd call me a coward?' Michael asked calmly, raising his dark brows.

'You know I would not!' The answer was quick, emphatic, Peter shrugged his shoulders and sighed. ' 'Tis of myself I speak; of the life I lead here.'

Michael walked a little away from him, bending briefly to pluck at dry grass; twisting it between his fingers. He lifted his eyes across the shimmering water, his back turned to Peter as he stood, legs apart.

'D'you not think it grieves me everyday?' he asked, his voice soft and low. 'I care for the King, for my country, as all honourable men do. In all the years I've spent moonlighting to the French Coast I've learned its line like my own hand. But then I see Rosalie. I consider the happiness I have.' He turned his head to look at Peter. 'Can I tell her that next week, next month, she may be a widow, or as good as if I were captured by the French? Has she not suffered enough in those months when I was exiled to the sea? Do I not owe her my freedom...indeed everything I have?'

He regarded Peter thoughtfully, then his mouth twisted into a slight smile. ' 'Tis the smuggling you miss, Young Peter. You've too much liking for a dangerous life!'

Peter pulled a face. 'And can you take me to task for that, Michael Pendeen?' he asked lightly.

Michael laughed. 'Indeed I cannot. 'Twas that love of adventure made me leave my father's farm and seek my fortune in a smuggler's boat.' He sighed, came back and placed a hand on Peter's shoulder. ' 'Tis over Peter. We've made our money at the smuggling game. We've four good ships and the pilchard seine to earn an honest wage. I'll put no more fear of revenue men in my home. Rosalie shall live with an honest name at least, even if 'tis not the gentleman's name to which she was bred.'

Peter smiled, turning his face away. He would never forget the look on Michael's face when Rosalie had admitted to running the smuggling ring in his absence and had shown him the account book which she had so meticulously kept. He had been absolutely stunned to learn that whereas he had believed he had lost everything, there was actually enough money to purchase more boats. The months since Michael's return had been good. Peter had enjoyed building up the business, taking an active part in all its aspects. But now he was restless. At nineteen, he was a man, a gentleman's son who needed the thrill of danger. And whatever Michael said he would have it. Michael called his horse; swung briskly into the saddle. 'You're a grown man now, Peter,' he said. 'Whatever you do it is your own choice. But promise me there'll be no flit by night at least. If you must go to war, then tell us before you do.'

Peter nodded. 'Aye. If I should decide to fight the Frenchies. There'll likely be press gangs around again soon. If I do go then it'll be on the vessel of my own choosing.'

Michael kicked his horse gently and turned her towards home. 'I'll see you at supper,' he called, quite certain that Peter would sail. But he must talk to Ben, Peter might be man enough, but at nearly fifteen Ben most certainly was not. And he would stay at home this time if he had to be tied to the bed...

Later that evening, Rosalie picked up her six-month-old son, Matthew, and held him close in her arms. For three whole months there had been a calm in her heart. There had been freedom from the dread that news might come suddenly to her of the arrest of her brother Peter or her husband Michael. There was still danger when they fished the treacherous Celtic Sea, but even Peter had been well taught and Michael knew the seas as well as any man.

Now, Peter had told them he was to find a ship which was working as a privateer for the king. She had looked at Michael with horror; seen understanding in his eyes, then she had fled to their bedchamber to sob.

Michael followed, came in silently, closing the door behind him before encircling her in his arms.

' 'Tis not so terrible, my love,' he assured her gently. 'He's not the reckless lad he was and I fear his mind is made up.'

Rosalie pulled away from him and sank miserably down onto the blue-cushioned sofa. 'He could have such a good life here,' she said, her voice full of tears. 'He could marry some girl of good breeding and set up house. When he's twenty-one there'll be the money my father left in trust for him. He'll have enough to start his own business if he wishes. But no...' she sighed with exasperation. 'He has to go to war, and... Oh, Michael!'

The baby woke in her arms and whimpered a little, Michael smiled and took him from her. 'This son of ours must not grow like his father?' he said with humour. 'When I was Peter's age I hardly saw land for more than a day in a month except it be French soil and loaded with kegs.' He laughed and tossed the baby gently into the air. ' 'Twill be well if the next one's a maid, then we shall have one land-lubber at least.'

Rosalie stared at him, a paralysing sense of alarm steeling her heart. 'You would not go, Michael,' she cried. 'You would not go as well?'

Michael laid his child down in the soft blankets and set the cradle rocking gently before he answered. Then he came back to her and leaned his arm on the back of the sofa, his mouth very close to her ear. 'I've not lost my love of my country, nor my honour, Rosalie. But I will not go to war, and I would not decide it without your agreement, for I love you more than either.'

She laid a hand quickly on his; he took

it and raised it to his lips. How could he leave what was still so amazing to him. That he, a Cornish peasant, should have wed a lady and given her such a healthy, handsome son. No, he could not go to war, yet he admitted only to himself that there was a little envy in his heart.

TWO

Captain John Trewarda eyed the letter he was given with suspicion. The young man who had brought it to him was too well spoken for his liking. Yet the letter said quite clearly that he was a good seaman, especially so it seemed in the use of the sextant and in navigation of the Cornish coast. And Michael Pendeen had written that letter. Few men would have their options valued as did the only sailor among the Pendeen brothers, and John Trewarda had many times known what it was to rely on his skill.

He lifted his head and stared hard at Peter, his eyes narrowing to dark slits on his hard, unshaven face.

' 'Tis no job for a woman,' he warned.

'I've not come to this lightly,' Peter replied. 'I've seen fire from the revenue boats many times, I doubt the Frenchies take better aim.'

The Captain nodded. 'I'll take 'ee then, tomorrow at dawn. There'll likely be room at the Inn if you're in need of lodgings for the night.'

Peter thanked him and took up his bag. There was food enough for six men which Rosalie had packed, but he'd want a bed tonight, the last maybe for some time.

Getting the lugger ready for sea took three whole days and getting rations aboard took the fourth. Peter was restless, eager to get under way. Then at last the canvas was set; he sailed as mate on the mid-day tide with twenty-eight others, destined for the shores of Alderney where they would take on further supplies. Rain splattered down on the decks as they glided south east from Plymouth. The westerly blew itself out for a while and the ship swayed gently, becalmed for two miserable hours. The delay was irritating to Peter.

When at last they had sailed, he felt a tremendous uplift of spirit, a feeling of excited anticipation as he saw the English coast slipping away.

Now a breeze was forming, a slight northerly which they could use well. They trimmed the sails and headed towards the sinking sun. As Peter glanced up at the sky, his gaze was held in wonder. The clouds rose from the horizon like mountain peaks, edged with silver until they reached a pool of glowing scarlet.

'Ship, Ahoy!' The call from the crow's nest tore his eyes to the south. A merchantman swelled her canvas with the same fickle breeze. Peter gave the order to alter course and they bore towards her with early triumph speeding their pulses. The ship sported an American flag, and she was carrying cargoes to France. Peter glanced once more at the radiant heavens. The sun was setting fast; they had not long to stalk their prey. The clouds spanned the sky now like a great crimson fire, whose smoke floated southwards across a vast, insipid blue. The merchant ship had seen them. She hoisted more canvas and prepared to run. Time was on her side. The hour of day was on her side. Peter sent for the Captain from his cabin below. Together they sent their lugger scurrying after that retreating fluttering rag.

The light went suddenly, as if the sun had fallen off the edge of the earth. The sky was grey, tinted with pink afterglow and useless. They were near, so very near, but without light they would come too close to the French coast to attack. They were within a short distance of Alderney;

the merchantman making for Cherbourg. John Trewarda heaved a reluctant sigh; the lugger turned towards Alderney and lay off her shores for the night...

In Northern Brittany, the River Penzé wound its way through the district of Léon to the sea. Less than a mile from its banks on the outskirts of the small town of Châteaunoir, Seigneur Jacques de Chauvelin, attired in a heavily embroidered, scarlet coat, paced incessantly backwards and forwards across the carpet of his elegant salon. His sixteenth century château stood supreme amid his acres of farmland and wooded slopes. A land where stone crosses arose in every corner, where small chapels were to be found in the most unexpected places, in the middle of a cornfield for example, so hidden, that when the corn was high, only the tip of the roof could be seen. A country where stone cupolas and porticos deck every other building and where wayside shrines are as numerous as the scores of Breton Saints.

Châteaunoir, so named because of the masses of dense thicket which covered the surrounding hills, and cast black shadows down into the valley, had been a peaceful town. But now there were signs of unrest, there was evidence that members of the armeé révolutionaire had been successful in their propagation of the Revolutionary Government policies.

Jacques de Chauvelin stood motionless for a moment against a background of richly coloured tapestries.

'*Non, Non, Non!*' he shouted. 'I will not release La Ville. He shall pay his dues to me as he has always done. What do you think I am, Nicolette?' He waved a contemptuous arm.

'You are a blind old fool, Jacques. Why do you consider it is you who are immortal when so many have already gone to the guillotine,' she complained loudly.

He turned away from his plump, red faced wife with irritation. Bad temperedly, he straightened his wig. Had he not always been fair with his peasants? Why should they revolt against him now? He had been like a father to them, providing the sharecroppers with not only seed but also the tools they needed, and often the loan of his horses for the plough.

Other Seigneurs had been too hard, of course, raising their tenants rents and dues until the poor sharecroppers had little produce left for their own use. But had he not, only last year, provided them with a new mill to grind their corn? Was it not enough that he no longer gave judgement in the Manorial Court, and that he had lost the exclusive right to hunt and fish on his own land. Why, only last September the General Maximum had fixed the basic prices of food to help the poor.

'You place your daughters' lives in danger for the sake of your pride,' Nicolette de Chauvelin persisted. Then she sat down suddenly, tears streaming down her puffy cheeks.

Her husband stood quite unmoved, with his back to her, then hearing a stifled sob he swung round sharply. 'Stop that at once,' he warned her coldly. 'You know I cannot endure a woman's tears!'

Her head bowed low, her lip trembled and her black fan flutterd to and fro across her face. 'We shall be killed, Jacques, I know we shall be killed!' she cried out, losing complete control and sobbing loudly.

Jacques de Chauvelin turned away in disgust. He resumed his pacing, his hands clenched tightly behind his back. The doors flung open suddenly and a young

24

woman burst breathlessly into the salon. She stared for a brief second at her sobbing mother, then ran over to her father and pulled at his arm.

'Tonight they have a meeting in the market place, Papa!' she told him urgently. 'Marie was in the town, she came straight back to tell me!'

'So they are having a meeting,' he shrugged. 'Zut alors! They are always having meetings. C'est rien! Do not concern yourself.'

'But she heard your name, Papa,' his daughter gasped in despair. 'It is the sans-coulotte!'

'And do you consider they would dare to come here? *La belle affaire!* My people enter without an audience! Pfft!' He threw her a sideways glance of ridicule, took out a silver snuff box, and placing a little onto his lace frilled wrist he inhaled deeply. When the exercise was completed, he looked back at his daughter and scowled. 'Go to your room, child, and you too, Nicolette! I will not have you consorting with the servants on such matters.' His voice rose to a high pitch, soaring a little. 'As for La Ville.' He looked up at the miniature of Louis XVI which still hung

25

defiantly over his bureau. 'Well, I will consider it again in the morning.'

Louise Theresa Gabrielle de Chauvelin made no attempt to sleep that night. She had accompanied her mother to her bedchamber, tried to comfort her, then sent for her maid to help her with her toilette. In her own room she had begun immediately to make preparations.

During the past months, she had been inclined to agree with her father. Their peasants were loyal, if not to the Royalists, then at least to their Seigneur, the head of the family to whom they had been subservient for so long. But then Marie, her maid had brought her copies of *Courir de Paris et Versailles,* and *Feuille Villageoise.* Louise had read them with horror, learning for the first time of the rapid spread of the terrors of the Révolution. Life in her beloved France had become suddenly sinister and frightening.

With astonishment she had listened to Marie's tales: prisons crowded with nobility, the heartbreaking wait for the roll call for 'Madame Guillotine' that occurred every day. The situation she learned, had worsened since the Jacobins had gained power a few months before. Throughout the country, anyone who was not a professed member of the local Popular Society lived in fear of arrest on the orders of comité révolutionaire. Doctors, lawyers, all came under surveillance, all were liable to sudden détention.

Marie explained how the newspapers were read out to the illiterate inhabitants of Châteaunoir, by paid readers, men chosen by the advocates of each particular newspaper. Louise had heard of the extravagances of Queen Marie Antoinette, the sumptuous, expensive gowns she wore and elaborate hairstyles. Her love of dancing and gambling had echoed around the country, causing the shaking of heads even in the farthest corner of Finisterre. Her death had caused little grief among the Seigneur's wives. Few had the carte blanche where their couturière was concerned. At Château de Chauvelin an astute head was needed to prevent a deficit in the finances. Louise's father was not over-generous with frivolities. She had been told, of course, of the execution of the King and then of his Queen, but her father had intimated little more. He refused to discuss it, shrugging it off as something which only happened in Paris and the largest cities. The Royalists, he considered, would soon have these impudent fellows in chains.

Marie had brought the newspaper to Louise hidden in a rough, cloth bag. She used this now as she packed a few necessities. Where she would go, for how long, these were questions she could not answer. She chose only black gowns, taking a pair of scissors and stripping them of their fine lace. Then she dressed herself, frowning sadly at the plain blackness in the mirror, and donning finally a white, broad-stringed bonnet.

Ruefully, she surveyed the few silks and muslins in her dressing room. How she loved these beautiful clothes, how she loved to dress before riding in the carriage...she remembered suddenly the sans coulottes; the people who it was said, walked everywhere, the people who had no chaise to ease their journeys.

She put away the rich gowns sorrowfully. What of the future?...she did not know. The joy she felt as she grew, as she discovered the new pleasures of being a woman. The prospect of being courted by some handsome young man had delighted her...she had already attended two of the Seigneur's Balls which were held every year.

The revelation of her country's turmoil had come like a stab from a knife. She had been so unprepared, so naive in her knowledge of life, that to be suddenly faced with the horror of death had at first formed panic in her young mind. Then she had calmed, become practical of necessity, and survival for her family had become paramount where happiness had once reigned.

Purposefully, she took the key of her jewellery casket. She possessed no money; she had never had any need of any. How easy it had all been, her dressmaker had always come to the château, as had the jeweller, and for that matter every tradesman they ever required. This had ended now of course, they had of late, been obliged to send their own servants into the town to purchase even the largest of items. Affectionately she fingered her jewellery when she had laid it out on the velvet cloth. She sighed with sadness, many of the items had belonged to her great-grandmother. Perhaps this was all unnecessary; her father could be right. But she shook her head and began sorting the items in front of her, for once, she believed the word of a servant, more than that of her own father. And Marie had warned her to plan her escape before it was too late.

She placed a gold engraved necklace back into the box with two matching gold bangles and a pearl brooch. It must not look as if she had prepared for this flight, they must be thought to have run away in fear.

Her thirteen-year-old sister Marrietta was sleeping peacefully when Louise entered her room; a tall candle flickering in her hand. Methodically she repeated the actions she performed in her own room, then she awoke her sister and bade her dress in the black gown which was laid ready on the bed.

Marrietta stared with dismay. 'But the lace, Louise,' she cried loudly.

Louise clapped a hand over her mouth then held her close in her arms. 'We may need to pretend to be peasants,' she explained in a whisper. 'We will go at dawn before even the servants are awake.'

The dogs started barking, suddenly they were growling, snapping, shattering the silence of the night with their discordant racket. Then silence again, abruptly silence ...a howl...a single bark, then silence again. Louise listened; willed her ears to hear more. An owl hooted in the trees...a voice? Did she hear voices? She crept near to the curtain, blowing out the candle. Nothing...not a sound. She came back to the bed where Marrietta was sitting petrified.

'What is it, Louise? For what are you listening?' she whimpered hardly daring to speak.

Louise placed her arm around her. There was a half moon whose light threw only pale shadows across the room. Then a smell, a faint, strange odour filtered slowly into their nostrils. Louise lifted her head and sniffed the air. The wind must have flared up the logs in the fireplace in the salon below...her face grew older in that minute of her life. At seventeen, she had been sheltered even more than most. But Louise knew in that minute, that the odour that now grew stronger every moment was not the confined logs in a stone walled grate, but the beginning of a fire that would destroy her home and everything that had been her life.

She crept to the window again, easing back the velvet enough for her to see out. What she saw there drained every touch of colour from her terrified face. Below the window, scattered across the lawns; crowding on the terraces were men and women from Châteaunoir. They stood in silence watching the château, and those in the front carried either pikes or sabres. Louise had never seen pikes before, but she had read about them, she knew well enough what they were for. As she knelt at the window, her heart went cold with fear. It was too late, already it was too late.

A murmur, a small rumbling chorus... then suddenly a shout 'She's going...' Then 'Liberté...!' 'Vive La République!'

On the terrace walls, on the faces of the people flickered the light of flames; almost hidden now by the rumbling of the crowd was the crackling sound. It was too late, escape was impossible. The Château was burning and their executioners waited like the reapers for a hare.

'Mademoiselle!...Mademoiselle!...' Marie's urgent voice broke into the room. 'Come, vite Mademoiselle. Bring the little one, follow me!'

Louise grabbed up their cloaks and bags; they followed, numb with shock. Suddenly their father was on the stairs, shouting for servants who had long since gone.

'Come, this way,' Marie told them

quickly, leading the way towards the kitchen.

Madame de Chauvelin was following, bleating at her husband to come with her.

'Where are you going?' he demanded. 'Are you mad? Do you think I will run away from responsibilities. Where are those damn servants? Zut alors! What do these fellows think they are doing, shouting in my gardens at this time of night!'

Louise released her sister's hand and ran back up the stairs to her father. 'Papa!' she begged. 'The Château is on fire. The men want to kill us. Are you staying here to let them do it?'

Her father regarded her with anger. 'I should have known you would believe all that rubbish, Louise,' he said.

So there, Louise left him, standing on the stairs. Marie was calling her and she hurried to join her at the entrance to the cellar door. It closed swiftly behind her and she stood on the flagstones waiting for instructions from her maid.

The women shivered and blinked as they came out amongst the black trees in the grounds of the Château. Louise had not even known of the existence of

33

the passage they had taken. Her mother seemed amazed as they stepped out into the ice cold darkness. Louise looked at her now standing trembling in her nightgown, clutching her robe together at the neck.

Poor Maman, she thought, always so dominated by Papa and now to be brought to hiding like a common criminal. She began to unhook her own cloak but Marie put a hand on her arm.

'Non, Mademoiselle, Madame may have my cloak. You will have need of your own. The night is bitter. Soon, I shall be in my own bed.'

The words could not have been more profound. They had escaped from the angry mob, but where did they go from here? She glanced back at the Château. Flames shot through most of the windows; black hurrying figures behind them at times. No doubt some of the contents would be thought useful by the peasants. In the distance they heard voices shouting, sometimes cheers, so far away that they seemed unreal and Louise began to wonder if she was dreaming it all.

As they stumbled onwards through the tall, shadowy trees, she pictured her father standing on the staircase, still insisting that there was no danger. She felt no pain for him, it had been his choice to stay. She had no respect for him now even if he were dead. Above them the night sky glittered with stars.

'Where are we going, Louise! Where are we going?' It was her mother's voice, begging, pleading as she gripped Maria's cloak around her and stumbled blindly through the November mud. Never in her life had she walked on ground like this. 'Louise,' she pleaded. 'Why can we not get the chaise? Que deviendrons-nous?'

Marie cast a look of scorn at her deposed Mistress. 'Because, Madame,' she growled. 'The sans coulottes are in the stables.' Feeling they were far enough away now, she lit the lantern.

Louise was thinking, desperately searching her brain for a place to go, accounting her friends, or those she had thought she had. Their relations lived too far away for any help; it was likely anyway that they were in the same situation. She knew that her father's brother who had been a Count, had been killed. On his horse, her father had said. She knew now that was a lie. She had seen his name in the 'Courir'. He had been guillotined like so many more. She

35

had wondered at the time why her father had made no claim to his title.

Marrietta slipped unnoticed from her mother's side and reached for her sister's hand.

'Could we not go to Monsieur Renoir, Louise,' she whispered. 'He was always so very kind. I am sure he would tell us what to do.'

Louise frowned at first, then the more she thought about it the more she realised what a sensible idea it was. Monsieur André Renoir had been their tutor until a few months ago. Then she had foolishly confided to her mother that she thought he was in love with her. Two days later, André Renoir had been dismissed. Her father had accused him of making advances towards his elder daughter. Louise had been humiliated. Never in all the time that he had been in their employ had he behaved other than as a perfect gentleman. Her pleadings however had been ignored. Monsieur Renoir had bidden her goodbye politely.

She had not seen him since. What he must think of her she knew not. That he would help, she had no doubt, but if he was in a position to do so was

36

another matter. Whatever Marie had in mind would put both her and her relatives at risk. Louise called her name.

'I have a plan, Marie,' she told her. 'How far are you going with us?'

Marie hesitated. 'I will go as far as you wish, Mademoiselle,' she said. 'But to be truthful it would be better if I returned home soon or I will be missed.'

'Then put us on the way to Le Pont Nord, Marie, S'il vous plait.'

Marie frowned, puzzled.

'I shall not tell you where we are going, then if you are asked you can say truthfully that you do not know.'

Madame de Chauvelin arrived beside them puffing and blowing. 'We do not have to walk any further, Louise, do we? I cannot take another step. Have you a carriage waiting somewhere for us, Marie?'

Louise scowled at her mother. How could she be so naive? 'Marie is leaving us soon, Maman,' she told her firmly. 'It is not safe for her to come further. We must go on alone. There are many fields yet for us to cross. I fear you must be very brave and walk many more kilometres.'

Madame de Chauvelin let out a small

gasp of dismay. She had not enough breath to say more and she saw anyway that her daughter was determined. As she herself had no plans, no idea at all, she would have to be glad that her daughter seemed to know what she was doing. She was beginning to wish she had stayed with her husband. To have died in the Château would have least have spared her this intolerable walking.

There were signs of dawn, when, totally exhausted, they reached a small cottage on the eastern side of Châteaunoir. Louise bade her mother and sister remain hidden, then she walked doubtfully up to the door and knocked softly. A window opened above her head, and the voice that called down gave her a surge of hope.

'Who is it?' he shouted, straining his eyes in the grey light.

'It is I, Monsieur Renoir,' she whispered. 'Louise de Chauvelin.'

She heard his gasp of surprise, his quick, 'One moment!' Then he was unbolting the door, holding a candle to light her way.

'My mother, my sister,' she said hesitantly. 'They are with me.'

'Then fetch them quickly,' he said. 'I will light a fire to warm you.'

He left the door a little ajar, and when they crept inside he was busy with kindling and flint. They closed the heavy door quietly behind them, so glad to be inside once more. Madame de Chauvelin sank totally spent onto a hard wooden chair. 'Je suis à bout de forces,' she gasped, then her head fell forward onto the table, and within seconds she was sound asleep.

André Renoir asked no questions. The fire was lit and Louise and Marrietta sat one on either side of the fireplace, holding out their hands, stamping their feet, and wondering if they would ever get really warm again. A cautirade was put over the now blazing fire and within minutes they were tasting fish and potato broth. Louise knew with relief that her decision to seek out this man had been right.

When André Renoir sat down at last, his eyes surveyed her from her toes to the top of her untidy hair, his face lined with concern. He looked hard at the thick mud which embroidered her gown and cloak, and he did not need to confirm that they had no horse and carriage which needed concealing.

Louise glanced up from the glowing fire, her heart so grateful that her eyes were shining. She looked across to him, and in a moment, in his eyes, she saw that the foolish thoughts which had caused his dismissal from her father's employment, had not been so foolish at all. For those soft grey eyes showed more than concern, more than just compassion for a beautiful young girl, they showed he loved her.

THREE

Dawn came with the tide, *The Tavy* slipped into an Alderney harbour with pale sunlight edging her masts. Peter went ashore at his Captain's bidding with the specific task of gleaning gossip of France. He came back with little of importance to their cause. Howe was still holding Toulon and that included nigh on half the French Navy. Robespierre and Danton still held the reins of power and the guillotine had never worked harder.

After taking on more fresh water, fruit and wine, they weighed anchor and set sail on the wind of morning. For two weeks they voyaged, westwards at first then turning southwards along the coast of France, seeing little of consequence, feeling only disappointment.

Peter wrote a letter to Michael: 'I have had the good fortune,' he wrote, 'to find a suitable ship. Tell Rosalie I am in good spirits, and I shall expect that nephew of mine to be talking fluently by the time I return.' He would hand the letter to some home-bound ship, but how soon he did not know.

Another two weeks and no incident of worth, and *The Tavy* returned to Alderney for rations.

Peter was restless, longing for action, the everyday work on board was no more than he had had on Michael's fishing boat. His eyeglass scoured the horizon with zeal. That so many French ships were held captive in Toulon accounted undoubtedly for the lack of French action. It was rumoured that they had insufficient crews to man those that were left.

Half-heartedly scouring the Atlantic coast of England, they had sailed northwards. On November 7th, a full rigged ship glided onto the horizon. Swiftly the captain gave the order to bear down on her to ascertain her colours. As they came towards her, portside, they raised cheers at the English colours they saw. Peter stood, hands on hips, watching as they came closer. Then he froze, stared for a brief second before relaying the order to change course.

The English colours slid briskly down the mast and the French Tricolour took their place.

As she came around broadside, three of her cannon belched black smoke and *The Tavy* shuddered as a ball caught her mizzen. The upper part of the mast split five feet or so from the tip; hung for a moment, creaking, before plunging down through the confused mass of ropes and spars, and catapulting off the gunwale into the swirling sea. Another burst, and grapeshot ripped through the mainsail. All hands were on deck by now; *The Tavy's* cannon boomed their answer as men climbed the main mast's rigging, muskets in hand. Slowly she turned, her stern gun booming as she came round to use the portside cannonry.

The French vessel veered away, but her captain was not on the run. His guns were longer reaching; they were eighteen pounders and when he came round broadside again, his next burst sent the helmsman clean over the deck with the wheel still gripped in his hands.

The young cabin boy, who was the Captain's nephew and who doubled as a powder monkey scuttled around from gun to gun, scrambling over fallen debris, his eyes smarting from wafting smoke and his head aching from the thunderous noise.

Men lay bleeding, groaning on the timbers, choking on the thick, black smoke which hung in the air. Splinters flew wildly, bedding deep into any flesh that stood, or lay in their path. Peter dragged a limp body from a cannon, and rammed powder home with a vengeance. He thrust in the gleaming ball, fired it, and watched it soar with excited anticipation. But it dropped dead in the waters between, throwing up a fountain of white, cascading spray. Their twelve pounders were out of reach. To have any hope of hitting their swaying target they had to close in. With no steerage, they could neither do that nor run. They were drifting, tossed at the mercy of wind and current. Drifting like flotsam, and of little more use.

A ball whined through the rigging, another found its target and *The Tavy's* main mast quivered, throwing yelling men from aloft to flounder in the waters below. The ship reeled, listed heavily to starboard. The deck swilled with colourless water which ran off red with blood. The mainmast, now stricken, toppled gracefully down, crashing through sails and ropes, splitting the deck, and John Trewarda's head.

Peter did not hear the cry. 'The Captain's dead.' It was drowned by the bellowing thunder of their own cannon, and the ripping of canvas as the wind gusted suddenly and took the scant sail that was left in its mighty grip, thrusting them nearer to the French ship. The sea broke high on the poop deck as *The Tavy* fell into a trough, came up again and righted herself miraculously just in time. All around, men were jumping into the swelling water swimming to pieces of floating wreckage and holding on in a desperate pointless hope.

Glancing at his Captain for orders, Peter saw only the blood and debris. The decisions were his now. Another round of double shot and they were near enough to damage her. His brain threw questions, answers; jumbled views on life and death. Their ship was dead. She'd go down in a matter of minutes, and this sparse crew with her, for the boats were shattered. A cannon broke loose from its lashings, careered across the deck, splitting the bulwark.

A last dying crack, all the starboard cannons? They might take the Frenchies down with them. A chance for honour; yet a struggle for survival. He wanted more than his nineteen years. Surrender and they would live, prisoners but they would live. The English flag flashed before his eyes, the crown; the dignity of honour. Then he saw Rosalie smiling, laughing. He thought of the girls he had kissed and the ones that were to come. Love of life triumphed. He signalled to the French vessel, and shouted above the raucous noise to the remaining men. Then he busied himself with the wounded all around him. The boatswain lay groaning by the poop ladder, blood gushing from his side where a sliver of wood from the falling mast had pierced him. Peter grabbed out his own shirt tail, tore off as much as he could and folded it into a thick pad before pressing it hard over the wound. Then he closed his eyes as the sea came over them, soaking the cloth with stinging salt.

It was strangely quieter now. He could hear the boarding party arriving now the cannons had ceased. He could hear the moans of men in pain and the wheels of the still rolling cannon. On the heaving, pitching deck, he waited for the French longboat, and the irons that would keep him below in the French ship's hold.

There would be little prize for the French Captain, only more men to be added to the already overflowing prisons of France.

Peter listened with care when they were marched onto *Le Guerrier's* decks. The Captain spoke to him in French. He answered misunderstandingly in English watching the faces around him. The Captain made no reply; he had not understood. Hoping to turn the fact to his advantage, Peter spoke politely to the Captain in French, near perfect French as he had been taught by his tutor at his childhood, Nottingham home.

The Captain looked surprised; threw back his head and cracked a laugh. 'We have an English Frenchman,' he declared with great humour. But Peter was still ironed down with the rest of his crew.

A brief, last glance at *The Tavy* before he was ordered below had shown her on fire. A lamp must have fallen; the spilled oil would soon spread. Flames shot upwards, disintegrating rope and sail like melting ice. He saw the first of her sinking, stern first, and heard the sizzling roar as the flames were snuffed by the pounding, swallowing waves. He did not see her last dying shudder; a musket was poked into his ribs and *'Allez!'* growled into his ear. He wiped a hand over his smoke-blackened face, saw blood covering it and wondered wearily if it might be his own. Then he descended the ladder with a deep sigh of failure.

There were other prisoners already below in the hold. It stank! He had expected that. The men were too close together; their poor rations scarcely kept them alive.

It was later that evening when Peter received a visitor.

'The Captain wants to see you,' the French sailor mumbled, making no effort to hide his displeasure as he undid Peter's irons.

The Captain was about to commence his supper in his cabin and much to Peter's amazement, he was cordially invited to sit down and eat.

He thanked the Captain politely. 'You are a generous man, Monsieur,' he told him.

'You interest me!' his host declared without lifting his head. 'What do you do when you are not playing at fighting wars?' he asked, his voice verging on scorn. He had a black, pointed beard and his small eyes gleamed like an eagle with its prey.

Peter thought how apt it was that his nose was so hooked. 'I've fishing boats, we own a Seine for pilchards and have our own salt houses,' he answered truthfully.

The Frenchman raised his brows, lifting his black chin so that he looked down at Peter along his eagle's nose.

'And for that, you speak such excellent French,' he rebuked him suspiciously.

Peter smiled disarmingly. 'I had the good fortune to have an excellent teacher, Monsieur, a Frenchman would you credit? He gave me the love, not only of the language, but also of the works of Voltaire, and the plays of Moliére.' He watched the Captain's face closely; saw his eyes light up with interest. He was visibly impressed; unknowingly Peter had struck a point in his favour. The Captain himself was a great theatre lover when he was ashore. It was a common thread, an opportunity which Peter would certainly not let pass.

The night in irons was terrible. Peter's hope that his supper with the Captain might have rid him at least of those was not realised. All it did was to earn him the ridicule of those men below who had eaten no supper at all. He had managed to secret some salted cod and dry biscuits into his pockets, and he offered them to the man beside him now.

'Frenchie lover!' the man breathed, spitting in his face and knocking the food to the deck where it was devoured at once by the ship's scraggy cat.

Peter lay down as best he could, trying not to hear the jeers and biting remarks of the men around him. For a moment he was tempted to tell them his plans, to explain to them that he hoped to gain the Captain's confidence, then trick him into gaining their freedom. But how could he trust them? There was not one amongst them who would not sell that information for a good meal, and he could not blame them.

Sighing, he closed his eyes. What sort of fool was he, thinking he was going to fight for his country and ending up in irons in a French brig? Around him were only hostile men. The wounded lay groaning, attended only by a boy with a cup of water. Above him creaked the timbers of an enemy ship. Below him the angry waters of an ocean black with night. What a fool he was to think his freedom such a carefree chattel.

Morning came, bringing aching limbs and back, and the grim knowledge that there might be little food today. As daylight thrust its way through the small portholes, so determination was born anew and hope grew by its side, bounding in leaps when he was taken on deck at an early hour to find the Captain at the helm.

'*Bon jour,* Monsieur the English Frenchman,' he called still amused by this personal joke.

Peter returned the greeting and joined him warily. Glancing around he saw only the faint shadow of land in the distance. They had been heading south east in the Celtic Sea when last he had managed to check their position. Squinting against the morning light, he strained his eyes trying to place the land. Lundy Island, that was it! They were sailing south west of Lundy. He glanced up at the sky, at the glaring November sun that shone down on them. Had he been fishing that day, he would have been warned to get his catch home before the late afternoon cooled the air. When the sun went, there would be mist, perhaps even before that. His eyes slid up the mast, they were flying the English flag again, hoping to lure some unsuspecting English seaman into the eagle's claw.

'The Kestrel Rocks!' Peter shouted

suddenly, pointing ahead of them. 'The Kestrel Rocks,' he repeated. 'You are heading straight for them! You do not know these waters, Captain!'

The Captain looked understandably started. Peter took his chance; he grabbed the helm which the Captain relinquished with surprising willingness.

'Regardez!' Peter shouted, pointing at white foam ahead. 'They are Judas rocks, hidden completely when the tide is like this.' He sighed, very loudly. 'It is fortunate I was here, Monsieur. We would surely have been wrecked. Perhaps you would allow me to take your ship safely along this coast. It is of course for my own skin that I fear.' He watched the Captain's face with interest. There was doubt in his eyes, the dawning of mistrust. Yet he was obviously not familiar enough with these waters to know that the Kestrel Rocks were pure invention. He did not answer. He glared instead at the distant coast, then back at his eloquent prisoner.

'You can of course chain me to the helm,' Peter suggested, 'and if you leave a man, you can change my directions at will.'

The Captain nodded, very slowly. 'Oui,

Monsieur, the English Frenchman, and I can shoot you if I please. You can take the helm of my ship, but beware, I shall be watching you!' Like a hawk, Peter thought, but he did not say it aloud.

The sky had paled a little by mid-day. He kept the ship well out to sea; light wisps of mist began floating across the deck. How tempted he was to take her round suddenly and head her for the shore. It was only the gun in the belt that prevented him. For unfortunately the belt was not his own. His guard was of a much heavier build than he, with thick black hair and matching teeth. How near they had come to Port Isaac; then to Padstow, although the tide had not been right for crossing the Doom Bar. The mist was thickening, hanging grey and silent over the ship. A tankard of hot grog was sent up to him and he drank it gratefully. Somehow he had to be at the helm when they passed the Scillies.

'I could do with some food,' he volunteered hopefully to the man who had brought him the grog. 'It is a clear run now.'

The man came back sullenly a few minutes later and escorted Peter below to the Captain's cabin. Once again, he sat down to eat. He wasted no time, a little careful boasting and he had the Captain verging on an acknowledgement of admiration. The large chart on the table had caught Peter's eye straight away. His mathematical ability enabled him to plot courses with remarkable accuracy. In his pocket was a small compass, an expensive gift from Rosalie. By the end of the meal the Captain was very impressed. His admission that his mariner's compass had been damaged was greeted by Peter's grave expression of sympathy. Inside he was laughing, what more could he want than misty weather and a broken compass...

When the last of the Scilly Isles vanished on the horizon, Peter was back at the helm. The mist had deepened, and the faint moon was hardly visible. After half an hour it had vanished completely.

Peter glanced at the man by his side. 'The moon does not wish to help us,' he said with a shrug. Inside he gloated. 'What is your name?' he enquired of his sullen companion who leaned idly on the rail.

'Claude Leblanc,' came the reluctant reply. Claude Leblanc shuffled from one foot to another, bored with his task of guarding this Englishman; disgusted at the friendship that seemed to have been allowed to grow between his Captain and one of the enemy, whom he would as sooner put a bullet through than watch.

'How long have you been at sea?' Peter asked, wanting to get him into conversation.

'Since a boy,' came the answer, then a silence when he descended the poop ladder and crossed to the bulwark amidships.

'The wind is changing,' Peter called, turning the helm while the man had his back to him.

'Oui,' Leblanc agreed, and his prisoner smiled in the dim light of the lantern that hung on the forkel. The wind was due south as it had been for hours. It was the ship that was turning, and Claude Leblanc had not noticed. The remainder of the turn was simple, easing her gently round at a wide angle, calling the sail changes as he had for hours checking his own compass in secret. The wind was little more than a strong breeze. The men were not enamoured of Peter by his constant call to trim the sails. Soon they could rest, he thought, for his turn had brought them nearer in line with the wind. If only the moon would keep itself hid. Even a man of such doubtful intelligence as Leblanc would notice if the moon were on the wrong side of them.

'We can use this wind now for a speedy run to France,' Peter observed amiably. 'We'd better have the spritsail rigged.'

Leblanc smirked as he passed on the order. Did this Englishman think he was to escape prison in France?

Peter watched agile shadows move forward across the deck to the forecastle. When they loosed the spritsail to steady the head, the wind took it with a vengeance. The ship ran before it, retracing the course she had just sailed, bound northwards, up the Atlantic coast of Cornwall.

Peter was immensely pleased with himself; he had timed it so well. Another careful turn before dawn and they would have land to port and the light of dawn on the correct side of the ship. The land to port would be the land of France, or so he hoped the crew would suppose if it were far enough away. It was a gamble, a terrible ploy of chance, but if it worked, he would be taking this handsome ship into Penzance before his captors realised that it was not Brest.

A mellow glow burst across the lower deck at four a.m, and the Captain appeared from his cabin, gripping a swinging lantern. He had been drinking heavily with the rest of the crew on the previous evening; his gait even now was affected by more than the swaying ship.

He looked hard at Peter. 'You have not slept, Englishman!' His words were slurred and indistinct. 'You will surely fall asleep at the helm.' He let his red eyes wander out to sea, narrowing them as if he hoped to recognise this part of the black, tossing waters; listening to the swish and splash of the waves.

'We have made good time, Captain,' Peter told him. 'Very soon you will see the coast of your country. By dawn we shall see the shores of Ouessant.' He could not remember any distinct difference between the coast of Ile de Ouessant, and the islands of St Martins but it was the best he could do.

The Captain raised his brows a little surprised. This Englishman was even better at his navigation than he had supposed. He revelled for a moment in the prospects of a comfortable bed, well cooked meals and a woman, then he took out his watch. 'You will rest awhile!' he announced putting a hand on his own brow, and gripping the taffrail for support. He took a deep breath through clenched teeth and closed his eyes as if he was in pain.

Peter frowned, needing any excuse to stay on deck. He knew the Captain had little faith in the navigation of most of his own crew for he had said so. 'To be truthful Monsieur, I would as soon stay here as find sleep. I'll wager there'll be time enough for sleep in those prisons of yours. 'Twill be hard enough for a man such as I who is used to breathing salt air. Would you grant me the honour of taking your ship at least as far as Finistére. Then you will be wanting a pilot to take her into harbour.' The Captain grinned. His head seemingly improved. He folded his arms with satisfaction. He could go back to his hammock with a clear conscience. This man seemed only too eager to do his work for him. With a promise to send up another tankard of hot grog he went below.

Peter sighed with relief. Claude Leblanc had been replaced on watch by another man. He was more talkative and easier on the eyes. But mercifully he was no brighter.

Dawn brought only mist and Peter sent up a prayer of thanks. It was only a light mist. They could still just make out a rugged coast, but that it was the coast of Cornwall and not that of Brittany occurred to none of the Frenchmen. They came close to St Martin's, a little too close for Peter's liking, but rain came in the mist and the view was obscured. He began working out what he would do when the Captain sent ashore for a pilot. He would have to swim, he thought. It was a fair way to Treen, if he had the chance he might take a boat. He wanted to warn the authorities, especially as there were English prisoners aboard. If the ship was sunk, he would not care, but the men in irons would have no chance at all.

The rain came faster, and he pulled his collar further up his neck. He was cold, very cold from the night on deck. He rubbed one hand stiffly on the other.

'Soon we shall see, Point de St Mathieu,' the Captain said with a deep sigh, appearing heavy-eyed and apparently still with a painful head.

Peter did not enlighten him to the fact that soon he would see Land's End. Ile de Ouessant, faded on the horizon despite its reputation for perilous currents and reefs. St Martins and the other Islands had fortunately the same notoriety. The Captain was frowning. He glanced over the stern taffrail, then looked up at the sky. A sideways glance at Peter then he walked forwards quickly to the forecastle, calling one of his men to his side. Something was the matter! Peter searched his brain. What was it? Something had put doubt in the Captain's mind. He returned to the helm almost immediately.

'Where did you say we were, Englishman?' he demanded roughly.

'Why, off the shores of Breton, Monsieur, of course,' he told him using the French for Brittany.

'And we have just left the waters between Ile de Ouessant and Finistére?'

'Oui, Monsieur. You can...' He did not finish. The Captain thrust his fist under Peter's chin and held it there.

'Then tell me, Englishman. Where are the Islands, the small ones through which we must pass to reach Point de Mathieu?'

Peter swallowed hard. There was nothing he could say. The largest of these islands was perhaps no bigger than St Agnes. But the fact that he had forgotten them might cost him his life.

A curt nod from the Captain, and the man at his side took hold of Peter, pleasure gleaming in his cold eyes. His arm was thrust roughly behind his back and a pistol pushed hard into his side.

'Allez!' a voice commanded.

'A moment,' the Captain demanded abruptly. He lifted his hand and brought it heavily across Peter's face. 'You think I am a fool, Englishman. That I would not know the shores of my own country from yours.' He hit Peter again, then kicked his shins like a child in a rage. Peter clenched his teeth, bearing the pain as best he could. He knew only too well that it was not that he had thought he could make a fool of the Captain that was infuriating him, but that he had almost done so.

The hold was ten times worse than before, because now he saw no hope. There would be no second chance, he must sit there, his legs pinned to the deck, whilst the Captain crossed the Channel; for the second time!

André Renoir was a diplomat. He had no sympathies with the violence and the bloody executions of The Terror, but nor was he willing to profess himself a Royalist and put his own neck at risk. When he had obtained the post as tutor to the two daughters of Seigneur de Chauvelin, he had thought himself extremely fortunate. Later, he considered it more of a millstone, but finding work after his dismissal had been suddenly eased by the death of Châteaunoir's school master. Like the de Chauvelins, André was a protestant and had been accepted for the vacant post as a further blow at the Catholic Church who had previously controlled all schools.

For him, now, there was school in the morning and private tutoring in the afternoon. Many of the Bourgeoisie were wanting their own children to be better educated. To have ones own personal tutor was considered extremely desirable, even if one could only afford half a day a week. Work was to be found, provided of course, he changed his teaching to suit the beliefs of the parents of his pupils, and expressed no extreme opinions himself.

Mathematics had seemed a fairly safe subject, then the calendar had been changed. He had worked out his own day index immediately, marking off each day of the new, Year One. He sensed that on the whole, employers were in favour of the recently introduced ten day week, those who worked the nine days were less enthralled by the idea. There were no Sundays, for this day and all feast days associated with the Church had been abolished. As for many others, working on Sunday still gave André pangs of guilt. He saw by his Revolutionary Calendar that it was the 30th day Messidor, Year One, but in his heart he could not forget that it was still the 20th of November 1793.

He was deeply aware that things here in Brittany had not been as bad as in many parts of the country, but after the burning of the Château de Chauvelin, it seemed inevitable that there would be more use made of the guillotine that stood so threateningly in the market square of the large town nearby.

Walking from his home this misty November morning, he had to pass the Church of St Dominic. He stopped abruptly by the Southgate and slipped inside the richly ornamented gateway. He had heard raised voices, strangely eerie amid the grey, floating mist. For a moment he concealed himself behind

63

the great stone Calvary, watching. Above him rose the life size statue of Christ, and kneeling around it, twenty carved figures of Saints, each one beautifully fashioned from local stone by men of Châteaunoir. He breathed a whispered prayer; how odd, how terrible it was that the sons and grandsons of those ardent craftsmen should now be so bent on destroying the Christian faith.

Carefully, he raised his head above the carved stone; what he saw made him sick in the stomach. Approaching through the mist was René Lefévre the local watchmaker. On the pike he brandished with such flagrant pride was the severed head of Father Benedict. Around him, becoming clearer every minute was a crowd of followers, their faces lit with gladness, their voices raised with joy.

André turned away, ashamed to call himself a Frenchman, and afraid that he might be seen by the murderous rabble.

Father Benedict had been a great friend, for although they did not share their religion, they had much in common in their knowledge of literature. Together, they had often discussed the Révolution in their beloved France. He remembered vividly, Father Benedict's words even now, or perhaps especially at this time.

'My Saviour died on the cross for me,' he had said. 'If it is required of me I shall die on the guillotine for him.' He had not even had the honour of Madame Guillotine, he had been slain by a rebellious mob because he refused to relinquish his faith and worship the Goddess of Reason. Even André, a non Catholic, had been shocked to hear of the closing of Notre Dame; shocked to hear of the Feast of Reason which had been held there. Dechristianisation it seemed had reached his own town.

He touched the small wooden cross that he wore at his throat, now hidden beneath his shirt. Would he dare to keep on wearing it now? Had he not enough problems hiding members of the Aristocracy in his own home?

Cutting back into the town by another route he reached the school for this morning's lessons. That afternoon, he made his way to the home of Francois Delarue on the Place de L'Apport, whose son he was required to educate on two afternoons a week. Jean-Francois Delarue was a difficult boy, more prone to exhibitionism of his acting talent than to serious study. But with a father who owned the largest theatre in Brest, this was hardly surprising.

The performance for the moment was 'The Cid' and Jean-Francois greatly fancied himself in the rôle of the hero. Less patient than usual, André Renoir lost his temper with the boy several times, and eventually his raised voice attracted the attention of the boy's doting father who burst suddenly into the room.

'Citizen Renoir!' he cried in an elaborately affected voice. 'I have a guest in the next room. I really must ask you to refrain from this raucous admonition of my poor son.'

The subject of his defence smiled sweetly, and widened big, brown eyes. 'He is always shouting at me, Papa,' he pouted.

André Renoir bowed his head in submission. 'I apologise, Citizen Delarue. Perhaps I have been a little impatient this morning.'

Francois Delarue let the corners of his mouth curve graciously into a smile. 'We will say no more, Citizen,' he said. 'I think that perhaps, Ma petit chou would prefer to come with me to meet my guest. He is the Captain of a French ship, Jean-Francois. He has just returned from the coast of England where he took forty prisoners aboard. If you are a good boy, I am sure he will tell you of his adventure and how clever he was to catch these Englishmen.

'Will they have to stay in prison, Papa?'

'But of course, and some are here in our own prison.'

He gave a short laugh. 'Just consider, ma petit chou, Citizen de Chauvelin will have to share the prison with these Englishmen. Is that not a great joke?'

The boy laughed, mimicking his father.

'Seign...I mean Citizen de Chauvelin?' André let the name escape his lips unchecked. 'He is in the prison?' he asked, forcing delight into his voice.

Francois Delarue nodded slowly. 'Oui, Oui. He was arrested last night when the sans coulotte burned down the Château.'

'Then his family are in custody, too,' André offered on a note of pleasure.

'Mais, non. The daughters and the mother escaped. A search is still being made for them.'

André said nothing, then a tight smile moved his lips. 'If you wish to meet this great sea Captain, Jean-Francois, then I will excuse you for the remainder of the afternoon. Perhaps if you consider me ill-tempered today, we should start anew tomorrow.'

'*Oui, Citizen!*' Then in a flash, he was gone.

André Renoir retraced the steps to his home with care. He walked slowly with none of the urgency he felt in his heart, dropping a coin into the bowl of a blind beggar who sat by one of the many stone shrines on the way. Yet he could hardly bear to wait for the moment when he would open the door and find that Louise was safe. He was also a little afraid, perhaps they had searched his house already, what if they were waiting for him now. He remembered Father Benedict. Impulsively, he touched the cross at his throat, but he did not tear it off and throw it into the bushes as he had first thought. He lifted his eyes to the heavy, gunmetal sky and asked God for protection for the girl he loved...

Louise watched guardedly from the window as he approached the cottage. She had spent the morning as he requested hidden in the bedroom with her mother and sister. He had left them books and food, and had found clothes for Madame de Chauvelin which had belonged to his mother. The cottage had been built by André's grandfather. The roof came down steeply on the eastern side. It had been with slight amusement that André had explained to them that the secret cupboard built into the eaves space behind a carved chest had been made to store grain and vegetables. A way of hiding some of the produce of the land to escape payment of dues to the Seigneur, Louise's grandfather. Now it was to be her hiding place.

André closed the door with a breath of sheer relief and ran up the stairs immediately. It was cold in the house and he shivered a little. He had not dared to leave a fire lit when he was at work for the smoke would indicate that someone was there. How he wished that it had been his habit to do so.

Madame de Chauvelin looked totally displeased, never in her life had she suffered such discomfort. She really thought it most intolerable that a mere schoolmaster should dare to treat her so. Louise had had great difficulty in keeping her mother in the room. She had spent almost the entire morning trying to get her to understand the risk that Monsieur Renoir was taking by merely allowing them into his house.

'You are cold!' he said as he came into the room. 'I will make you some broth and light the fire. Perhaps if we are careful you could come down stairs now. But it is most important that you stay away from the window.' He remembered suddenly that he had news for them. The murder of Father Benedict had so dominated his thoughts that he had almost forgotten. 'Your husband, Madame de Chauvelin, he is in the prison. His life has been spared at least for the present.'

She burst into tears. They were unsure as to whether it was with relief or sorrow, but no-one cared to enquire.

'Can we go to visit Papa?' Marrietta asked eagerly.

Louise looked at André Renoir in sheer desperation. Had she spent the morning in explaining everything for nothing?

'You will, I fear, be unable to visit your Father, Mademoiselle. It is with deep regret that I must tell you quite plainly that they are searching for you.'

Louise's eyes widened in dismay; her young brow lined with worry. 'Then we must leave your house immediately,

Monsieur Renoir,' she said quickly.

André Renoir looked tenderly down into her worried eyes. 'You will stay, Mademoiselle, until I find a safe way for your departure.' He left the bedroom to go downstairs but she followed him quickly. He lowered his voice so that only she could hear. 'Do you not think I would willingly go to the guillotine if I thought it might save your life?' He looked away from her at once, afraid that he might say too much. 'The matter is settled.' He touched her hand and felt how cold it was. 'Come down now. The fire will warm you. I shall put potatoes in the oven for later.'

'You are very kind, Monsieur,' she breathed softly. 'I shall never be able to repay you.'

He smiled briefly, before hurrying down the narrow, winding stair. A thought, an answer to the problem had just occurred to him, and it was so amazing that he hardly dare let it free in his mind.

Louise observed carefully as he lit the fire, then put on the kettle to make coffee. He had taught her many things; the Theorem of Pythagorus, the appreciation of not only French literature but also the works of English writers like Shakespeare.

She rememberd how beautifully he had read 'The Seasons' by the English poet James Thomson. Now he taught her to lay a fire; to light it. The safe way to place a kettle above it and then how to scrub potatoes and place them in the oven beside the fire. There was no merit in expecting her mother to make such an effort. She had done little else but shed tears and wring her hands since their fortuitous escape. Marrietta must learn these things, too, but she was too young to take any responsibility. Louise knew her place in this terrible new world. She accepted it with courage. She must somehow become what the peasants would call the breadwinner and support her family.

It was much later that evening when Louise once again found herself alone with André Renoir. Her mother and sister were asleep upstairs in the huge box bed that was André's. He had offered to sleep downstairs in the kitchen. Louise could not sleep and had come down in the hope of a warm drink. André was awake, and reading, he made her warm milk and watched her thoughtfully as she drank it.

'I have jewels with me, Monsieur, valuable ones,' she said at last. 'If only

I could sell them I could give you money for our food.'

He smiled. 'I need no payment, Mademoiselle Louise, and it is likely you will need the money yourself.' He picked up his own cup and held it warming his hands. 'The food I can offer you is so poor. Of truth, I dare buy little more than I would for myself without bringing suspicion on this house,' he confessed sadly.

Louise gasped: 'You must not give us your own food!'

He gave a short laugh. 'Then am I to eat whilst you go hungry? Do not concern yourself with this. It is the market tomorrow. There I shall be able to buy a little more without causing raised eyebrows. I shall also seek more news of your father.' He sighed. 'I regret that I can think of no way of helping him, nor at the moment I fear, a way of selling your jewels.'

Louise lifted her face to meet his. 'It is enough that you do already, Monsieur. How I dislike imposing on you so.'

For a moment his eyes held hers, then he sent up a prayer for strength to resist the intense desire he had to take her in his arms. It would be so very wrong, perhaps even disastrous. There was only one thing for it, he must put his plan to her then abide by her decision.

'There is one way in which I could help you much more,' he began.

'You know how we could escape from France?' she gasped.

'A solution which would enable you to stay in France, and be safe,' he told her, suddenly eager.

She frowned, not understanding. How he hated to see those lines on her lovely brow.

He stood up, facing her, standing very erect. 'I have, you will agree, shown you nothing but respect and humble service, Mademoiselle Louise.' Then he went on. 'Yet I am certain that you are aware that my thoughts of you are...to be blunt, more than those of a mere tutor.'

She held her breath; the morning of his dismissal still vivid in her mind; the shame she had felt at bringing it upon him still troubling her conscience.

He touched her arm, just lightly; she recoiled away, suddenly aware that she did not want him to touch her.

He breathed in deeply. 'If you were...to become...my wife—' He hesitated, amazed to hear the words coming from his own lips, 'then there would be no more danger for you.'

Her eyes faltered, fluttered away from him to the glowing fire, then back again to look nervously into his.

'Monsieur Renoir!' she whispered, thrown completely off balance by this, her very first proposal of marriage. 'I could not, I would not dream of letting you make such a sacrifice for my benefit.'

'But Mademoiselle, how could it possibly be a sacrifice for me? It is not because you are in this unfortunate position that I ask you to be my wife, but rather that this situation allows me to do what I would have otherwise thought impossible.'

'But you must think me a child! I have but recently left the schoolroom.'

His brow deepened, then he mustered a smile. 'Mais, Oui. Once you were a child to me. I am older, a full ten years older, I concede. But is this any reason why we should not marry? Once you were my wife, you would hardly notice the difference in our ages. Surely, Mademoiselle, I am not an old man. I am barely twenty-seven years, and to me you are certainly no longer a child. You are a very beautiful woman.' She had looked away from him; he followed her gaze around the plain room; looked down at the hard, slate floor, at the wooden settle. For the first time, he saw it through her eyes. 'I would not expect you to live here,' he assured her quickly. 'I could get a position in another part of France where we are not known. Louise, Ma chere Louise! I love you!' He moved towards her again and she saw urgency in his face. Then he changed, suddenly he was her tutor again. He crossed to the fire and threw on two logs. Then he knelt down by the stone hearth, his head bent low. 'Pardonez moi, Mademoiselle. I have no right to ask such a thing of you.' He turned, rose slowly to his feet and stood facing her. 'You need have no fear. I will still help you to leave France if this is what you wish. Do I not remember that you have a cousin in England?' She nodded, but said nothing. 'Then I will do my best to find a ship which will take you to safety, though I confess my knowledge of them is very poor.'

He saw confusion in her young, bright eyes. His unexpected outburst had startled her. He smiled, trying to give her reassurance. 'In some way we shall find a ship.'

She nodded again, not daring to smile lest she should encourage another declaration of his love. 'I had thought that I might go down to one of the harbours,' she said at last. 'Surely one of the seamen would be willing to take us to England for payment of a diamond necklace?'

He shook his head, sat down at the chair at the table. 'You must not consider even leaving this house, Mademoiselle,' he told her earnestly.

'But I would not be recognised!' she exclaimed.

'And do you have le Carte de Civisme, with any other name but Louise de Chauvelin?'

She shook her head sadly, then she smiled a little shyly, feeling at last that she could trust him again.

'Thank you for the honour you have done me by asking me to be your wife. I do not however think it would be the right thing for me, or for you.' She clasped her hands together and sighed. 'I can see that we are to be a great trouble to you. If only these people would just let us go away freely, we would do so. But they are set to take our lives, when I cannot see that we have done them harm.'

'You have never done anyone harm in your whole life, Louise de Chauvelin!' he told her sternly. 'But the people of the Revolution see you only as an aristocrat, and to them, that is...' He stopped abruptly, hearing a sound outside the window.

It was only a faint noise, a barely perceptible sound but it made them sit motionless, listening with racing pulses. Then André moved, softly, carefully he eased a large book from a shelf and laid it open on the table. Perhaps it was only rain trickling down into the water butt; he prayed that it was.

'Into the roof,' he whispered. 'Quietly.'

Louise rose silently and crossed the room, then she crept up the stairs and waking her mother and sister she ushered them quickly through the hole behind the chest. When they were safely inside, she glanced briefly around the room and seeing Marrietta's cloak she grabbed it up before squeezing after them herself.

Downstairs, she could hear André talking. Had he let someone into the house already? For a second she listened, then allowed herself to smile a little as she took hold of the brass handles and pulled the chest tight back against the wall.

In the kitchen, André was pushing the unwashed cups swiftly away into a cupboard, leaving only his own on the table. He was still talking aloud. Quoting lines from Pierre Corneille's play Médée, changing his voice into a high pitched range as he leaned forward quickly towards the open book to check the words. He would have preferred to read Moliere's L'Ecole des Femmes, but it had been banned during the Revolution.

A loud hammering came on the door. He stopped speaking and closed his eyes for a brief second of prayer. Then he went slowly to the door. His hand was on the bolt when he remembered the cross. Rapidly, he slipped the chain over his head and let it trickle down into his boot. Then he pulled back the bolt.

'Bon soir, Citizen Kerbol,' he exclaimed as the door flew open and the lanterns outside lit the faces in front of him.

'Out of the way, Citizen Schoolmaster. We're going to search your cottage.'

He was pushed roughly to the side as six men crushed hurriedly into the small passage. He gave a short forced laugh. 'Certainement! But am I not to know for what you are searching?'

The last of the men took him by the shoulder and almost threw him into the kitchen. 'You know already for whom we search,' he growled. 'The women, the de Chauvelin women.' He waved an arm towards one of his companions. 'Citizen Bellay fancies the pretty daughter for a wife.' He smirked at André. 'You know the law. They are the property of the state now. Any court can award her to him if he asks.'

André swallowed hard. He glanced at Citizen Bellay with horror in his heart. This man was in his forties, a widower whose wife it was said had died from malnutrition and who had borne him eight children. He stood now, biting his nails, a gleam in his usually dull eyes. André looked away from him, feeling sick at the mere thought of him touching Louise. He had forgotten the law of the Revolution, forgotten that by it he too could have forcibly taken Louise to court and made her his wife.

He laughed out loud, more easily this time. 'You think I would hide those pigs here,' he cried incredulously.

Citizen Kerbol kicked his shin. 'Do not play games with us, Citizen Schoolmaster. We know they're here. Zut alors! We heard them talking. We've been outside a full fifteen minutes.'

André changed his face; forcibly he radiated amazement. Then he laughed again, found it surprisingly easy now for he was playing a part with every nerve in his body. 'You heard them talking,' he almost shouted. 'In here?' He looked suddenly at the table and pointed speechless at the open book. 'Look!' he cried, moving briskly to the table. 'Look!' he repeated running his finger along the lines. 'This is what you heard! Médée, Corneille's Médée. I have been reading this play, taking all the parts!' He looked hard into their disbelieving faces with cool, steady eyes. 'This is what you heard!'

Citizen Bellay scowled; laughed shortly. 'You think we'll believe a story like that,' he ejaculated.

André shrugged. 'Whether you believe it or not it is true. Citizen Bellay. I will show you.' He flicked back the page and began reading, changing his voice to falsetto for the parts of the women.

81

His so unwelcome visitors were obviously shaken. Citizen Bellay looked distinctly disappointed. Their profound belief that they had heard the voices of women was falling apart.

'We'll still search!' Citizen La Braz announced doggedly. He looked at his companions and scowled. 'I don't trust this schoolmaster. He's likely got them in his bedchamber.'

André closed the book slowly. 'D'you think I'd give protection to that cow and her daughters?' he asked quietly. 'It was she who got me dismissed from the Château. I ask you, Citizen. Am I likely to want them here?' He shrugged again. 'But if you must, search the house. Don't forget to look up the chimney, will you?'

The hand of three of the men were already stuffed into their pockets, their enthusiasm somewhat dampened. It was nevertheless a thorough search. When they came to the bedchamber, André bade them look into the bed. He opened the wardrobe door and held his candle inside so that they could see clearly. Then they trooped disillusioned down the stairs. He offered them wine, but they declined saying they would as soon get home to their own warm fires. One by one they filed out, bidding him 'Bon Nuit,' and their apologies.

André waited after they had left. For a full fifteen minutes he waited. Then he opened the oven and took out the tray of cakes that he had been afraid they would find. Then he climbed the stairs to his bedchamber and brought down Louise, Marrietta and Madame de Chauvelin to be treated to hot cakes and warm milk and a glowing fire.

FOUR

Peter lay in despair on his prison bed. Time was dragging so slowly that he had come to counting beetles on the walls. He had been pleasantly surprised by his room of confinement. It appeared that the French prisons were so overcrowded that large houses of the aristocracy had been taken over to supplement the existing buildings. He was fortunate enough to be held in one of these, the mansion which had given its name to Châteaunoir. The conditions that his brother, Ben, had described from his short residence in a French prison were certainly not in evidence here. The room was airy, shared by only two other prisoners; the food could undoubtedly have been worse.

The town itself was small; a smattering of unpretentious streets, clinging to the hillside, and criss-crossed by dark, narrow passageways. Rows of meagre cottages were punctuated at intervals by an elegant, lantern roofed house with black painted, wood frame and white, plastered walls. Carved figures adorned the frontage, standing like soldiers in tiered rows. Clematis and pennyworts, asleep for the winter filled crevices on dank walls. Peter was not impressed with Châteaunoir.

His first impulse on arriving at the gaol had been to seek a way of getting a message to Michael. Michael would rescue him! In the hours that had followed Peter Harvey had grown from an adventure seeking youth into the man he wanted to be thought. Why, after all should Michael risk his own freedom, even his life for someone who had made his own free choice. A choice to go to war, despite the fears of his sister and the apprehension of her husband. No...if he was to escape at all, and that was the only aim in his mind, then he must do it himself. Able as Michael was, he could not be expected to be forever rescuing Rosalie's brothers from their self made plights.

The prison was well guarded, he could see that well enough through the iron barred window. He quite enjoyed playing the amiable, courteous guest; always careful to thank the turnkeys politely when he was brought food. A few days before he had made a request, but as yet nothing had come of it. Sadly, he had concluded that it had been refused by the Chief Jailor. As he lay now, willing the hours away, he heard footsteps approaching. It was not yet time for a meal so he thought it must be the arrival of a new prisoner.

The door swung open, a tall man with a crooked nose and beady eyes stepped in. A fumbling turnkey introduced him as the Chief Jailor. Peter sprang to his feet, apologising that he was on his bed when such an eminent person should deem to visit him.

Citizen Duval glowed a little, conceited pleasure flickering in his eyes.

'I understand you have asked for books, Englishman?' he enquired, giving a loud snort.

Peter smiled charmingly. 'Why yes! Monsieur,' he said in clear Breton.

'Citizen, if you please, Englishman!' the jailor bellowed.

'I beg your pardon,' Peter fawned.

'Why do you want books?' the man demanded, hardly allowing him to finish.

'Why because I like to read, Citizen. I thought perhaps some French literature, something that would enable me to learn more about your estimable country.' He concluded regretfully that all that little speech would get him was PERE DUCHESNE or FEUILLE VILLAGEOISE or some similar newspaper which would be an advocate of Vive Le Révolution! Even so there would be better than reading beetles on the wall.

'You read in both Breton and French?' the jailor was asking.

'But yes!' He saw some interest in those small eyes and pursued his favour. 'I like mathematics too. Anything that will give my brain work to do.'

The jailor let out a vibrant peal of laughter. 'I wish my son had your likings, Englishman. What is your name?'

'Peter Harvey.' He hesitated before saying more, seeing a thread, wanting to snatch at it before it was pulled out of his reach. 'Your son, Citizen?' he enquired. 'Am I to understand that he does not like his study?'

'Like it, he hates it! Two years he's spent at that school and still he can't read a word.'

'Perhaps he needs a little extra time, Citizen. Some of us are not so quick at learning as others. And school teachers have many pupils, they cannot spend

87

all their time with one. A little care, a few extra words of explanation and the slowest of pupils can learn. Not of course that I suggest your son is slow, Citizen. But perhaps he needs a little extra encouragement.' He sighed, shrugged his shoulders, and shook his head sadly. 'It is almost a pity that I'm in here, Citizen, for I would willingly help him if I could. My own young brother needed many hours of my help before he mastered the art of reading.' How Ben would thump him for that. He had been most insistent that he had no need of Peter's help at anything.

The jailor was considering, Peter could almost see the cogwheels churning around in his brain.

'If you could see fit to letting me have a few books, I should be most grateful,' Peter added deliberately.

Citizen Duval nodded curtly now, then he called to the turnkey to unlock the door and left without another word. Peter lay back onto his bed and hoped. The other prisoners in his room came over to him astonished. How dare he speak to the head jailor in such a familiar way? Did he not know that only the slightest misdemeanour in gaol could have one sent to the guillotine?

Peter smiled, yes suddenly he could smile a little. Great trees it was said, from little acorns grow. And he had planted a small seed. He only had to wait now for the sun and rain of thought to make it blossom. It might not make an oak tree, but a lavender bush would be useful just now.

On the following morning, he was escorted to the jailor's house. No reason was given for his summons; even Peter was beginning to think that perhaps his companions had been right. He was shown into a small room which sported a table and four chairs. A young Frenchman was already there, seated at the table, running his finger thoughtfully through the pages of a large book. He closed it and looked up when Peter came in, giving what was a most reassuring smile. For a horrible moment, Peter thought that this must be the jailor's son, but then he spoke and explained the situation.

'Good-Day,' he said quite amiably. 'I understand that you are willing to give Paul-Michel some help with his reading. And perhaps later with mathematics?'

Peter nodded, but said nothing.

'My name is André Renoir. I am the schoolmaster at Paul-Michel's school. I have been asked to bring you some books.' He smiled again and Peter began to relax. 'May I call you Peter?'

Knowing full well by now that the only alternative was for him to be called Citizen Harvey, Peter agreed readily. He wondered even then if André Renoir had the same dislike of this mode of address.

'You do not object to my offering to help?' he asked.

'On the contrary, I would be grateful. Paul-Michel, like many of my pupils, is lazy. As you have, I understand, already remarked, a little personal tuition can work wonders. Do please sit down, I realise the difficulty of your position. There is, I must tell you, a sentry outside the door. He will escort you back to your...er...room, shall we say.'

'Merci.'

'Your French is excellent, Peter!'

Peter grinned. 'I was taught by a Frenchman. Are these books for me?'

André nodded. 'Oui, a few for Paul-Michel, and I understand you asked for some books yourself. I will lend you some of my own. If they are not to your liking, perhaps you can tell me when we meet again.'

Peter thanked him. 'I was becoming a madman imprisoned in a room with nothing to occupy me but counting beetles and listening to the ravings of others. These will truly save my sanity.' He glanced approvingly through the books, noting with surprise, The Works of Daniel Defoe and Oliver Goldsmith.

André saw his lifted brows. 'We French are not all merely readers of the papers of the Révolution,' he said bitterly, breaking off abruptly as if he realised too late the implication of what he was saying.

Peter looked steadily into the grey, worried eyes. 'It is already forgot,' he assured him quickly. 'I hope we can be friends.'

André sighed, smiled and gave Peter his hand. 'Good luck with Paul-Michel, I hope you can do a better job than I.' He crossed to the door to call in the sentry. 'I have to be at the school in ten minutes,' he explained. 'You will start your teaching tomorrow. The guard will bring you to this room where you will find your pupil, eager and willing we will hope. Bon jour, Peter.'

Peter bade him 'Good Day', then he walked across the cobbled yard, an armed sentry at his back, but a spark of light lit firmly in his heart...

A heavy sky hung over Breton as Peter walked briskly back across that yard on the following morning. He had been awake early and had watched the dawn through those black bars. The dim light had barely lifted the leaden sky, streaking out below it as if it were trying to escape. Just like me, Peter thought, streaking out to the jailor's house, taking the first tender steps towards freedom.

Paul-Michel was a quiet child, sullen; withdrawn, suspicious of this blue-eyed Englishman, who, he had been told was going to make him work. Peter made no attempt to present him with the books on the first morning. He spent the time talking, trying to probe into the boy's imagination, to find an interest which could be expanded. When he began telling him about life at sea, about the battle with the French ship, he saw a light flicker in those too dull eyes.

He kindled it well with more stories of smugglers, telling the boy that this must remain a secret between them.

'Oui, Citizen Harvey!' The eagerness was profound.

On the second morning, Peter wrote out a few simple words. Words which meant more than white letters on a black slate. Words like 'La mere' and 'La Lunè', and the French words for ship, for keg and for gun. The battle of war had lit the fire, the battle of interest, of a desire to learn was yielding to victory.

By the end of the nine working days, Paul-Michel could read many words in French and speak whole sentences of the language now forced upon the Breton speaking people by the Révolutionary Government. Peter was encouraged, his father was more than that, he was delighted. On the tenth day, the day of rest, Peter was brought by the sentry to the jailor's house. To his amazement, he found that he was invited to dinner.

Towards the end of the lesson on the first day of the new week, a knock on the door heralded André Renoir.

'Bon jour, Peter?' he greeted him cordially. 'Bon jour Paul-Michel. I hear you are working hard.'

'Mais oui, Citizen Renoir. Will you hear me read?'

'But of course,' André sat down at the table expectantly.

The boy read the words he knew as Peter wrote them on the slate.

'Très bon, Paul-Michel, très bon. I see that Citizen Harvey has given you an interest in the sea.'

'Oh yes! Citizen Renoir, he tells me such stories, about the war, about smu...' he stopped abruptly looking up at Peter in dismay.

Peter laughed and patted his shoulder. 'I think your schoolmaster can join in our secret, but remember, no-one else!' He exchanged an understanding look with André, then went on. 'We have been talking about smuggling, about the terrible men who take kegs of spirit across to the shores of England and smuggle them ashore without paying taxes to the English government.'

André grinned. 'Ah, I understand. It is very interesting to learn words about this.' He got to his feet. 'It is time to finish now, Paul-Michel, time for your dinner. I wish to speak with Citizen Harvey before he leaves.'

The boy nodded, said 'Au revoir,' then closed the door behind him.

'I have more books for you, Peter.' André said as soon as he had gone.

'Thank you, the others are still in my room. I would have brought them back had I known you would come.'

André lifted his hand, gesticulating that it was of no matter. 'I will fetch those another day,' he said. 'I dare only stay a few minutes. I have a favour to ask.'

Peter was surprised, 'dare only', was this smiling schoolmaster putting on the act of good humoured confidence. 'I am not in the best position to grant favours, André, but I will gladly do anything for you that I am able.'

André nodded, solemn now. 'In the prison,' he said, 'there is a man called Jacques de Chauvelin. I would be most grateful if you could find out anything about him. Do you know him?'

Peter frowned, he had heard the name, but that was all. 'I will try, of course,' he said.

'I must warn you that he is an...aristocrat. Too much contact with him might be dangerous for you. I am almost surprised that he has not yet gone to the guillotine. He is not a bad man, foolish, stupid even, but not bad.'

'And you wish to know how he is, may I know the reason?'

'I think not. I put myself already in danger by asking this of you. And there are others.'

Peter nodded, hearing the sentry shuffling restless feet outside the door. 'You can trust me, André,' he said lowering his voice. 'Whatever you hear me say to these revolutionaries, if the truth be known I am more of an English aristocrat myself than the sailor I would have them believe.'

André eyed him for a moment, his hand resting on the table. Then he spoke, almost in a whisper. 'Then perchance we may help each other yet. I will see you in a few days. A visit too often may bring suspicion on either of us.'

Peter was intrigued by this unexpected turn in the conversation. His lessons with Paul-Michel continued to be fruitful which was greatly to his advantage. He was told that in future he would be given a written permit each day which he was to show to the sentry outside the prison before making his own way to the house. Added to this was the privilege of taking wine to the other prisoners; a great asset in his desire to find Jacques de Chauvelin. He found him two days later, alone in a very small room, huddled in the corner, sullen and unresponsive. Peter's efforts to get him to talk yielded nothing. After three such visits he condescended to say, 'Thank you' for the wine.

On the next occasion he poured out the whole of his story. The burning of the Château; how his wife and daughters had escaped, but for all he knew they had been murdered anyway. Peter said nothing to him about André Renoir's enquiries, he thought it likely that Jacques de Chauvelin would break down under the slightest pressure. He was not to be trusted with the safety of others and according to André there were others.

Peter waited impatiently for the school-master's next visit. He was able to leave the prison now by just showing the written permit. This, he was told would continue as long as he returned promptly at the allotted hour. The sentries collected the dated permits every day, or at least most of them did. With Peter's assistance, such as a timely comment about the weather, there was an occasional omission. In his pockets already he had two permits, out of date maybe, but they would come in quite handy in the near future, he was sure. And something told him that the time would depend on André Renoir.

The occasional invitations to eat at the jailor's house completed Peter's list of assets. He even doubted that the sentry was given any fixed time for his return. It also seemed likely that no-one had bothered to say on what particular days he was expected at the house. If he appeared at the gate with a pass, then the sentry let him through. Escape from these Breton shores seemed closer than he could have hoped.

André was guardedly pleased to hear the news of Jacques de Chauvelin, although it was much as he expected.

'You know the whereabouts of his daughters and wife I presume,' Peter asked him pointedly.

The schoolmaster's face hardened at once. 'What makes you think such a ridiculous thing as that?' he demanded curtly.

'Jacques de Chauvelin told me about them. I presumed that this must be the reason for your interest.'

'Then you assumed wrongly, Peter. I have no idea at all where they are, neither do I care.' He shrugged his shoulders, but to Peter's perceptive eyes, he had reacted too rapidly.

'And if I could escape from this place, then could I not be of use in escorting the ladies to England?' It was a risk, a calculated risk, but it paid off by the look in André's eyes.

'You would do that?' he enquired in a whisper, leaning his hands on the table.

'I would need a little help; a horse perhaps, somewhere to hide. I've many contacts in the harbours. St Pol de Léon would suit me well. It is near enough to Roscoff. A boat to Guernsey would see us safe on English soil.'

André was collecting his books together slowly, making a great pretence of seeing they were straight, for his mind was too obviously not on the act. 'I will return in two days,' he informed Peter. 'Perhaps you would like to read the Voltaire I shall send you, with great care. I shall place a message in the leaves. Guard your advantages well, my friend. I would not wish you to lose them.'

FIVE

Louise hovered nervously near the kitchen window at the home of André Renoir. It had been dark for an hour and still the sound for which she waited did not come. The doors were bolted and only the firelight lit the room, flickering shadows across the ceiling; crackling so much at times that she jumped up from her chair thinking it was footsteps outside.

The kettle began singing, whistling a high note. She folded a thick kettle holder and removed it quickly from the hob. For a moment it continued to whistle, then she lifted her head, her heart thumping in her breast. That was not the kettle now, it was the whistled tune she had waited for since dusk.

Silently she slipped into the passage, listening for a second at the foot of the stair. Her mother and sister had retired to bed early for which she had been glad. Slowly she slid back the bolt and eased open the door, peering around it as she did so.

'C'est moi,' a voice whispered and in the clear moonlight she saw a tall figure, somewhat dishevelled in appearance but with fair hair and the remarkably good looks that had been described to her.

'Come in,' she told him in a whisper, and Peter Harvey stepped into the narrow hall.

She closed the door and pushed the bolt home before she spoke again. 'In here, Monsieur. I cannot light the candles until Monsieur Renoir returns.'

Peter crossed gladly to the radiant fire; he had been hiding in the fields for hours.

'I was a little worried, Monsieur. It seems to have been dark for a long time,' Louise said self consciously.

Peter smiled. 'Dark, yes, but the moon had a ball. I gave up waiting for clouds in the end and decided to risk it. Where do we hide if anyone comes?'

'There is an entrance into the roof behind a large chest in the bedroom.' She hesitated a little before going on. 'It is a little difficult, Monsieur. There is my mother and sister also, you know this?'

He nodded, then put his hand inside his

coat and pulled out a large bottle of wine. 'Rather a nice touch, I thought,' he said with a grin. 'With the compliments of the Chief Jailor. Could you put it somewhere safe?' As he turned to her he saw her clearly for the first time, lit as she was by the dancing firelight. Never before had he seen such a beautiful girl, such appealing brown eyes and such clear, pale skin. For a moment, he stood motionless, just staring at her, then he remembered the wine and held it out, reprimanding himself for his lack of singlemindedness.

She placed the bottle quickly in a cupboard, pushing it to the back and hiding it with the pots and pans.

'The Head Jailor, he gave it to you?' she asked him incredulously.

He laughed a little too loudly and she put her finger to her lips quickly.

'My apologies,' he whispered, making a slight bow.

'How did you escape?' she asked eagerly, pouring the water from the kettle into a large pot for coffee.

He smiled, feeling suddenly justified in boasting. 'With today being a rest day,' he explained, 'I was not expected at the house. Sometimes however, I am given a pass to fetch wine for the other prisoners, or to have dinner with the jailor's family. I showed the sentry a permit which I was given several days ago and fortunately he did not check the date.' He rubbed his hands together close to the flames and grinned up at Louise. 'I walked boldly into the kitchen and asked for the wine for the prisoners. "Help yourself, Citizen" the cook called. "You know where it is." So I helped myself to a bottle of the best wine, then left the kitchen and slipped out onto the road by the side of the house. André had drawn me a map to find this cottage, and as I said I have been hiding in the fields ever since.'

'Monsieur Renoir said that we must expect that they will search here tonight. They will know that he spoke alone with you at the jailor's house and are bound to suspect him.'

Peter nodded, frowning. 'I have no notion when they will find me gone. I doubted the wisdom of my coming here, but in truth there is nowhere else I might go. It is well that the winters are mild in Breton, the prison was cold enough. I doubt I could survive out in the fields for long.' He sighed and shook his head.

'But André takes a great risk in having me here also.'

'Monsieur Renoir is very brave. He risks his life every moment that we are here.' Her brown eyes darkened with sadness, deeply aware as she was that the responsibility for burdening him so was hers alone.

Peter's heart lurched suddenly; he put out his hand and took hers without thinking. 'I am sure he is not the only one who has shown braveness, Mademoiselle. André has told me of your great courage.'

Louise blushed defensively. She had not met many young men, but the few who had visited the Château bore no comparison to this Englishman. Never, of course, with the exception of Monsieur Renoir, had she been alone with them. This Englishman was disturbing, yet she felt no fear in his company. One would never know that he had just escaped after weeks in prison, so good humoured was he; and how his blue eyes sparkled in the firelight.

Peter released her hand and turned his face towards the leaping flames when he saw the colour rush to her cheeks. She moved swiftly to the table and began cutting bread and cheese for him.

'You must be hungry!' she said in a matter of fact way. 'André will be here soon. He hoped to bring bacon with him.' She glanced at Peter and at once her eyes were caught and held in his steady gaze. For all of thirty seconds, some strange impulse passed between them, a fragile thread that tugged at their hearts and set their pulses racing. Then she dropped her lashes and he sighed silently with sheer relief, for he would have kissed her, he was sure he would have kissed her and only minutes had passed since their meeting.

She spoke suddenly in a small, quiet voice and he did not look at her again because he dare not. 'If you wish to sleep Monsieur, we have made a bed for you in the eaves.'

He shook his head. 'I will wait for André, and do not worry, Mademoiselle Louise, tomorrow I shall ride to St Pol de Léon. From there I shall find a boat that shall take us to English soil.' He sighed. 'With good fortune, with God's help we shall spend Christmas at my sister's house.'

She lifted the plate from the table, came over and put it in Peter's hand. Her eyes were shining, her face aglow with excitement.

'Is it possible?' she whispered. 'Is it true? Shall we really have Christmas in England?'

'Indeed we shall,' he assured her, quite in control of his emotions now, then he stood still, listening, before he put his hand on her trembling arm. 'Is it André?' he asked in a low whisper, close to her ear.

She shook her head frowning, then got silently to her feet and began slipping away the bread and cheese. Quickly, she slipped the drinking cups into the cupboard, then indicated to Peter that he should wrap up his own food in the small cloth which she held out to him. Then she crept towards the stairs, beckoning him to follow her. Unquestioning, he did as she said, for there was little doubt now, a crunching sounded on the path outside, whispered voices came to them as they crept on hands and knees up the bare wooden stairs.

Madame de Chauvelin was not pleased to be woken, but she climbed with only a little grumbling out of the great box bed and squeezed through the hole into the eaves. Marrietta was hardly awake and Peter almost carried her, lifting her gently in to join her mother. Louise was climbing into the bed, throwing the clothes over hurriedly and leaving the sliding doors wide open in the hope that it would soon cool the blankets. When she had checked the room she slipped quickly into the darkened space in the eaves and showed Peter how to pull in the chest to seal them in.

In the blackness, they sat listening. The voices were louder now. There was a bang as if someone was trying the door, then a loud crack and another. The absolute certainty of a search filled their minds now; soon there would be men in the bedroom, opening the wardrobe, lifting the lid of the chest as they had done before.

The last crash came and the door flew open; men's voices shouted in the kitchen below. Boots clattered on the stairs like an invading army of soldiers. Strong curses rent the air. Louise shivered, sitting on the floor as she was. For the first time she felt really afraid. Before, she had been so busy organising her mother and sister, now suddenly there was someone else to take charge of things. André had been there before of course, helping, providing, but André had been with the men when they searched, using his wits to their extreme.

Suddenly there was a scratching at her feet, a loud clawing at the wooden beams. Her hand flew involuntarily to her mouth to stifle a scream although she knew it to be only a mouse, a small, harmless thing. Immediately an arm came around her shoulders; she was pulled close against Peter's chest and held there firm and safe, until the scratching had ceased, until the thumping and harsh words had melted down the stairs again. Until the splintered kitchen door had been slammed shut in the disgust of failure.

Then they waited; still they waited before they dared to move. Peter stirred, pressed Louise's arm before letting her go.

'Christmas in England!' he whispered into her ear and she was glad of the dark, for no-one else could see the pinkness of her cheeks.

Chairs were upturned and mud splattered across the floor from careless boots when Peter at last ventured downstairs. He crossed quickly to the broken door. They had, it seemed, used a large log as a battering ram to break enough of the door to reach inside and draw the bolt. André had a key to the side door and would use this when he returned. Louise came down and began picking up the chairs, but Peter put a hand on her arm and shook his head.

'Leave them,' he warned her, speaking softly. 'They may return. They must not find it changed.'

She looked startled, her brown eyes widened in dismay. The prospect of another visit from the sans coulotte seemed too much to bear. He saw tears in her eyes now, the strain of the past weeks beginning to break the great strength of spirit she had shown. He hooked his finger under her chin and lifted her face so she had to look at him.

'I think it would be wise for you all to sleep in the eaves tonight,' he told her softly. 'With the door broken it would take them no time at all to get in again. Go up to bed now. I'll come, I'll help you with the blankets.'

He bent down a little towards her. 'I shall stay here and wait for André. There is nothing more for you to do, nothing more to cause you concern.'

The tears were flowing now, falling unchecked. 'But André...' She stopped remembering that she should not call him that. 'Monsieur Renoir should have returned long ago. I fear something is amiss.'

Peter forced a smile, much against the true feeling he had. 'I should think he is keeping out of the way. He may have seen that rabble on their way here.'

'Oh no, Monsieur. He would never stay out of the way!' She looked at Peter, her bottom lip trembling a little. 'He asked me to be his wife,' she confessed.

At once, Peter understood, he knew what that statement had cost her, and he wondered suddenly if she were promised to some highborn Frenchman, some man who was likely headed for the guillotine himself. 'You do not have to tell me he is concerned for you, Mademoiselle,' he assured her gently. 'I know it already from the way he talked of you.'

He smiled now as she began to wipe the tears from her eyes. He had thought to wipe them himself but a handkerchief used in a prison for several weeks was hardly the kind to use on a lady. 'Now,' he said, 'as Monsieur Renoir is not yet here, I must play your schoolmaster. To bed at once and sleep well, Mademoiselle Louise.'

She consented gladly, giving him a warm smile through her tears, a smile that set his pulses racing, and made his throat go dry.

Once the de Chauvelins were settled snugly with pillows and blankets in the eaves Peter allowed himself to worry. What Louise had inferred was perfectly true. André should have returned long ago. Friends had invited him to the coffee house to play cards. He had thought it wise not to refuse their invitation and Peter had agreed. But why was he so late? Was he drinking wine as well as coffee? What if such drink loosened his tongue?

Peter sank wearily down onto a chair by the fire. In spite of everything, how good it was to just sit by a fire and feel free. He sighed. Freedom, did he really have freedom? Sitting there listening for footsteps that might never come. The wind stirred, rustled the trees in the garden. It was louder now through the gap in the door. He sprang up startled, then he sighed again, felt the sheath at his waist that had been empty since he had been taken prisoner on the French ship. He glanced round the kitchen, saw the bread knife that Louise had left on the table, and picking it up he thrust it swiftly down into the vacant leather with a stifled yawn.

The hours crawled by and still André did not come. Peter had slept little on the night before, going over and over the details of his planned escape, seeking to foresee any obstacle that would prevent his clean getaway. Now, he was near exhausted. He sat limply, resting only on a hard wooden chair, desperately endeavouring to keep awake. The warmth from the fire, the need for sleep won the battle. His head fell forward onto his chest and he slept. When he opened his eyes it was to hear the door handle being turned, the creak of it opening, then footsteps and a curse before it was slammed shut.

There was no time to escape up the stairs, he cursed himself for sleeping when it was so important to stay awake. Instantly he flattened himself against the wall which adjoined the passage. The knife was drawn and held firm and ready in his waiting hand.

Someone pushed open the kitchen door, Peter sprang; had him gripped tight round the neck, the long knife pointed at his throat.

'Mon ami, if you do not release me, I

shall not be able to tell you where to find a horse.'

Peter dropped his hand, let go of André at once and heaved a deep thankful sigh. 'I fell asleep,' he said bluntly. 'I should have known it was you.' He frowned, puzzled. 'But how did you know it was me?'

André laughed. He looked tired, deep lines on his brow and dark patches beneath his heavy lidded, grey eyes. 'The sans coulotte carry their own sabres, Peter. They would not need to resort to my bread knife.'

Peter nodded, understanding. 'Where have you been, André? I was damned worried when you didn't return last night.'

André smiled briefly. 'With your friends, Peter. In the prison as you were. They have been asking me questions all night, keeping me awake in the hope that I might tell them where you were.' He sighed wearily. 'I think they believe me; at least I hope they do. I do not think I could stand another night like that.'

'Then the dogs did suspect you, they came here as you see.'

André nodded, letting his eyes roam around the chaotic room. 'I will repair the door first,' he announced. 'Then we shall make some plans together over coffee and bacon.' He yawned loudly, letting his head fall back. 'Then I shall sleep for an hour or two. But I must be at the school in the morning, even if I fall asleep with my head on the desk.'

Peter nodded. 'And tonight, we shall get a horse and I shall ride to St Pol de Léon.'

SIX

The moon was hidden in light cloud as Peter took the reins in his eager hands. The air smelt cold and the brisk wind cut sharply at his bare face and hands. He glanced behind him at the three de Chauvelin women with concern. They were huddled together under rough blankets in the mud splattered cart which André had 'borrowed' for the night.

It was André for whom they waited now. He was retrieving a parcel of food that he had hidden earlier on in the hedgerow. The lane where they were to begin their journey to Roscoff was quiet; little used. He was to come with them to the coast then return with the cart. Peter's ride alone to St Pol de Léon on the previous night had been a complete success. Anton Frére, the Breton fisherman who lived there had been at home, and had agreed readily to take Peter and the three unnamed ladies out on his boat on the following night. He would sail close in to Guernsey, landing them on one of the more remote beaches.

Peter bit his lip; rubbed his hands together, wishing André would hurry. Now, he came, passing up the bundle to Madame de Chauvelin, then clambering up beside Peter with a sigh.

'*Très bien, mon ami,*' he said. 'We can go. *Vive la lune,* providing she stays in the cloud.'

Peter smiled and glanced up at the sky before he slapped the horse hard on the rump with the coarse rope that played the rein. She started forward, easing into a steady walk. Total blackness would have made their journey near impossible for although cloud covered the moon, enough light filtered through to make the lane into a grey band between the huge, dark shapes of the hedgerows.

'Even the wind is right,' Peter observed as they drove along.

'The wind?' André frowned.

Peter laughed. 'For the ship, Monsieur Le Mâitre. We shall need wind, shall we not, to fill the sails if we are to reach Guernsey before dawn.'

André nodded, then pursed his lips thoughtfully. 'I have never been on a ship, although I have lived near to the

116

sea for the whole of my life.'

'Then come with us; I have asked you before. There would be no problem in finding you a post.' Peter glanced to the man at his side. 'What is there to keep you here in this insane country. You have no sympathy with the people who rule you, neither would they protect you. Come to England with us, you would be most welcome in my sister's house.'

André shook his head, and there was a sadness in his eyes that Peter could not see in the darkness.

'I could not leave the children, mon ami. Now, at this time I can teach them little of the love of God, of the things that are to me important. But the time will come; these men of violence; these men who blaspheme with every word they utter, they cannot keep this country in their clutches for ever.' He smiled, and sighed a little. 'The time will come when I shall be needed to teach the children of God-fearing Frenchmen again. I must not be found lacking in courage to stay because times are hard.' He glanced at Peter, sitting arms on knees beside him. 'If Louise had even considered my offer, if I had thought there was the slightest

117

glimmer of hope, for that I would have come.' He straightened up, moving his feet to a more comfortable position. 'No, mon ami. I must stay in France. You will take Louise to your sister. One day, she will find happiness with an English man.' He smiled, and laughed briefly. 'Perhaps even you, Peter. Perhaps you will find her desirable as a wife.' He leaned his head to one side thoughtfully. '*Oui,* this I would like. This would please me.'

Peter rapped the horse, making her go faster. 'I'll admit to nought of that,' he said in a whisper. 'I've many seas to sail before I think of marriage. And Louise will likely be wed to some English Lord by that time.' There was a surprising lack of conviction in the statement and André smiled to himself. Then his face changed; he reached into his coat as if he had just remembered something. 'A parting gift, mon ami,' he said, holding a pistol towards Peter. 'It is all I have but you may have need of it.'

Peter took the pistol and pushed it into his belt. He had shot at game on many occasions but never at men with such a weapon. He knew how to use it, most likely better than André, yet he hoped he would not have to use it face to face.

He thanked André, then they were silent for a while. The night around was silent with them except for the dull thud of the mare's hooves, and the creak and rattle of the cart.

'*Vive la République!*' The shout came suddenly in the still night. The horse reared, whinnying with fear; she turned so acutely at the resounding chorus that the cart almost toppled over. A small army of men were suddenly on the road. Perhaps ten, perhaps more. They stood with staffs raised around the cart. One had already grabbed the horse's head, keeping his hand firm on the bridle rope. Peter glanced behind. There were more men there, leering grins on their faces as the moon slid gracefully into full view, throwing white light at the high-hedged lane. Where they had all come from Peter could not imagine. There had been no sound, no sign at all of the slightest movement ahead of them, yet here they were imprisoned by this vagabond crowd. His hand caressed the pistol, but he did not draw it.

'So, we have them, Citizens!' a voice shouted in vibrant Breton. There was laughter, loud, raucous laughter.

'And all five of them, like rabbits in a snare!' someone else bellowed.

'Come on then, Citizen Bellay. Claim this de Chauvelin woman you want for a wife. Come on, don't be shy, there she is, a pretty wench I'll grant you.'

Citizen Bellay was pushed forward. André moved a hand towards Louise.

'Keep still,' Peter breathed in English. 'Do not show them you care!'

André was white, his hands were shaking a little. 'If he touches her, I'll kill him!' he muttered under his breath.

'With your bare hands?' Peter asked. 'What good could that do Louise. They're armed with sabres at least.'

'Come on, Citizen Bellay, come on!' The shouts grew more impatient, the men moved nearer.

Citizen Bellay was André's side of the cart, he looked uncomfortable, not quite sure what was expected of him. He looked up at Louise through hooded eyes, his boasting about making her his wife had got out of hand. By nature he was a shy man in company. He shook his head.

'Leave her in the cart,' he said with a facade of scorn. 'I can wait for her now. Let's get these dogs back into town before

I think of my own pleasure.'

A murmur of agreement filled the lane. André breathed, for the first time in seconds he took in the biting air and let it out with a sigh of immense relief.

'We'll not let the schoolmaster ride,' Citizen Kerbol shouted. 'Let him walk like the rest of us.'

'Oui. Make him walk, make him walk!' The cry went round like an echo.

Citizen Bellay reached up, feeling important now; grabbed André's arm, dragging him down so that he fell onto the stones below.

Peter cursed under his breath. He had hoped they would all be left in the cart, he had the rein, curled round his hand ready to strike the horse. Would they want him down as well? There was no feeling of cold now, his palms were damp with sweat.

'The Englishman, let's have him crawling, too!'

'Non! Non!' Citizen Le Braz put in hurriedly. 'I don't trust that eel. He's clever, that one. Let's leave him where we can see him clearly.' He lifted his head, his eyes scanning the horse. 'Keep the mare's head well in your control, Edouard! The rest of you keep close to the cart. Watch him I tell you, watch that English pig like you watch your wives!'

Marrietta was sobbing. Peter heard her now, then Madame de Chauvelin's voice reached him soft and comforting. 'Do not worry, my little one. They would not hurt a little dove like you.'

Peter scowled: Don't you believe it, he thought passionately. I wonder whose wife Marrietta was intended to be. His hand clasped the pistol now, but still he dare not use it. So many men and André held amongst them, a strong arm gripping each of his; if only they had left him in the cart! Peter wondered suddenly if any of the men spoke English. If not, it might be of use to him.

'Do these idiots know that they are fat and ugly?' he shouted, speaking in clear, purposefully slow English.

André responded. Peter heard amusement in his voice.

'They have the faces of monkeys!' he called back.

'Speak in Breton,' Citizen Kerbol screamed angrily.

Peter grinned. Not one of them, not one of these idiots had understood. He could at least talk freely to André and Louise.

The horse had been turned. The rein wrenched from his hands. They were moving slowly now in procession. Peter's mind flashed the description, funeral procession but he tossed the words away angrily, and took stock of the situation. One man walked on either side of the horse; others paraded like a guard of honour alongside the cart. André's escort walked behind, and Peter knew that his heart must be near to breaking. André would see no escape, he had not learned the twist of fate. Citizen Bellay had been lifted bodily onto the cart. He sat there grinning, enjoying his sudden fame, glancing every now and then at the white-faced girl beside him. Louise was silent, she had said, nor done nothing since the first shout had come. Peter could not see her face even if he looked behind him, but he knew her thoughts, he knew the terror that must steel her heart every time she caught a glimpse of Citizen Bellay's fat, self-satisfied face.

Peter searched his brain for any plan, for any thought that might grow into use. He had achieved the impossible before, could he not do it again?

He shouted again to André, ignoring the staff that was thrust hard into his ribs. 'Can you get to the cart if we can run?' he asked quickly.

'I will try,' came the answer. 'But do not wait for me. Go when you can, get Louise away from that pig for me, that is all I care.'

A sound followed that made even Peter wince. A muffled cry that escaped from André's lips as he was struck on the face with the full force of a wielded pike. Blood spurted from his nose and flowed unchecked down his face. He tried to avert his face, turn it away from Louise so that she would not see, but he heard a sob and knew with grief that she had been watching.

The lane narrowed now, the wiry branches of the hedge crowded the cart so that the men who walked beside it were forced to walk at the back.

If only André was in the cart...if only. Peter remembered a slight descent ahead of them, an incline that would help the horse with its weighty load.

His voice in a low whisper, he spoke over his shoulder to Louise. 'Move closer, Louise,' he told her.

'Yes,' she answered softly. 'I am here.'

'When I shout, now, you will push

Citizen Bellay out of the cart. You hear me, push hard.'

She answered, 'Yes,' but her voice was faint, and shaking a little. 'But Monsieur Renoir?' she whispered.

'You heard what he said, be ready to pull him up.'

'Yes, Monsieur, but he will not do it, it is too far.'

Peter gave no answer. There was none to give. He knew as well as André that the chances of his reaching the cart alive were less than slim. But they were possible, anything is possible; escape is always worth a try.

He undid the buckle that fastened his belt with the mere quiver of movement then rolled the belt in his hand and whispered. 'In a moment,' over his shoulder to Louise.

Citizen Poussin had moved back beside the cart, squeezing in by the hedge, guarding Peter with a supercilious smile on his face. Peter doubted he had any idea of what it was all about. He lifted his hand and pointed at the moon, speaking as if to the man by his side.

'Do not answer, Schoolmaster! Be ready,' he warned in a loud, clear voice.

The man nodded with an idiot grin, glancing himself up at the sky, thinking that Peter was commenting on the moon's brightness.

'Now!' Peter shouted, thrusting out his arm like a catapult and sending the startled Citizen Poussin sprawling into the hedge. Then he crouched up with his back to the nearside hedge, swinging the pistol round in a semi-circle and shouting in Breton.

'Any man who moves I will shoot!'

In the same instant Louise pushed, and Citizen Bellay fell heavily onto the road behind the cart, tripping up all four of the men who walked there.

'Run André, run,' Peter shouted.

André had thrust a hard elbow into the stomach of the man by his side, bending him double with pain. Now, he was running, darting from side to side, away from the arms that might grab out at him. A sabre flashed in the moonlight. André missed it by inches and saw Louise reaching down towards him. Peter shouted another warning. No-one moved, they all stood motionless, hands clenched on their weapons, waiting.

Swiftly Peter swung round to give a warning to the man to his right at the horse's head, then he spun back to watch André. Louise caught him, pulled his arm with all her might until he got his foot safely on the cart. Then suddenly he was up, breathless and exhausted, he lay in Louise's arms, his eyes closed as if he would treasure this moment all his life.

Another shout from Peter and he let fly with his belt. The horse lurched forward, neighing, tossing her head in the air, scattering the men who had held her firm until that moment. The bridle rope was loose, dragging on the ground, and as they passed the men it caught one of them by the foot and threw him somersaulting at the hedge. A thrown pike soared through the air, striking the side of the cart and vibrating noisily. The lane was so narrow here that there was scarcely room for the cart.

The horse was wild, wild with terror. Behind them figures ran, brandishing staffs, yelling and shouting at the top of their voices. Well aimed sabres clattered short on the still dancing pebbles.

André had sat himself up; his breathing less laboured, but his face still dark with blood. The figures behind were losing ground as the mare reached the slope and her load was lightened. Then a shadow appeared as if from nowhere, a dark shape lurched at the back of the cart. An arm reached in, took André by the tail of his coat and held on like shark's teeth. Louise screamed...Peter swung round, saw what had happened and fired. The man fell backwards, but his hand stayed clenched. As the cart moved forward, he took André with him, hard onto the road.

Louise screamed at Peter to stop, but he had no hold on the galloping mare. The men behind were spurred into action again, running, running after the cart, knowing now that the pistol was void. Peter shouted at the horse, but she paid no heed to him. Then André's voice came to him through the rabble of Breton curses.

'Go, mon ami, go. I die for her gladly, remember...' They did not hear him finish, the words were silenced abruptly. They neither saw nor knew whether it was a knife or blow, but André Renoir fell limply onto the stony earth.

The horse was galloping now, panicked by the pistol shot, flying away from the slowing figures who still panted in pursuit. They were clear away, rattling down the moonlit lane and heading directly back towards André's cottage, back towards the town they had tried so hard to leave. At last the horse was tiring. Peter shouted to her, calming her, until eventually she had slowed to a walk. Quickly, he jumped down and grabbed up the bridle rope which still trailed on the floor, then he climbed back silently onto the hard, jogging wood and wondered which way he should go.

He felt movement suddenly behind him, someone had clambered over onto the seat. He thought it was Louise and turned his head to look at her. Madame de Chauvelin glanced back briefly, her face deathly white, but in her eyes he saw a look he had not seen before. She had spent so much time feeling sorry for herself, grumbling continually at the indignations that she had to bear that neither he nor André had been able to feel much sympathy for her at all. Now, there was anger in her eyes, a hardness that came from hatred.

'You will need some help with your direction, Monsieur,' she stated firmly in French. 'Tell me which way you wish to go and perhaps I can advise you.'

'We cannot go to Roscoff,' Peter informed her, recognising in her an offer that was genuine, and already concerned by his scant knowledge of the countryside. 'We must turn off this lane as soon as possible. They will most likely get horses to follow us.'

Madame de Chauvelin nodded. 'We must then travel further by land,' she observed.

Peter slowed the horse a little, she would tire pulling her heavy load. 'Do you know Kérouzéré?' he asked her hopefully.

'The Château, Monsieur Harvey?'

'Yes. If you could guide me there I could find a small beach I know. There is a man lives near who might help us.'

Madame de Chauvelin was silent for a moment, turning the problem over in her mind. 'The next turn to the right, I think,' she said doubtfully, 'then right again after a kilometre or two.'

Peter listened to her instructions with only a nod. How he wished he could speak to Louise. He could hear her sobbing occasionally then silence when somehow he felt that only he could share her pain. He found the turn, and Madame de Chauvelin nodded her head that this was the one. As the cart trundled slowly around the narrow bend, Peter sat motionless, arrow straight in his seat, in the distance, he had heard hoofbeats coming behind them. He pulled the mare to a standstill and sat listening. Three white faces turned with his towards the corner watching with terror, for there was more than one horse and the sound was so near that it would be impossible to run.

'Into the hedge,' Peter breathed, half pushing Madame de Chauvelin from the seat and down onto the road. He sprang down quickly, ran to the back of the cart and lifted first Marrietta then Louise down beside him. For the brief second that he held Louise in his arms, he was overwhelmed by the strong desire to crush her to him and hold her there. He looked down into her tear-washed eyes and he knew that there was an understanding between them, and that she at least did not blame him for the tragedy of the man who had loved her enough to face death. Her lip quivered as he let her go, then a faint smile flickered across her face before she melted into the shadows.

Hurriedly, he clambered onto the cart again and walked the horse slowly on. Any attempt to hurry would invite suspicion. Louder now the hoofbeats came, reaching the corner and halting for a full three seconds before they came clattering down the moon-grey lane behind him. Closer, closer they came. They had passed the de Chauvelins; there was no uttered cry of discovery. Even now there was only the sound of the hooves; the creaking of the slowly rolling cart.

Suddenly, they were upon him, he sat rigid, moulded to the seat, the pistol drawn on his knee.

'Bon soir, Citizen,' a voice called, and two more echoed the greeting.

Peter lifted his hand; mumbled back an answer and watched amazed as the three horsemen cantered away, quite unconcerned that they had just passed an English escaped prisoner and his three aristocratic protegées.

The remainder of the journey passed surprisingly uneventfully. Once the castle at Kérouzéré was in sight, Madame de Chauvelin climbed back to join her daughters. A crimson band stretched across the eastern horizon. Above it hung heavy cloud bathed in hues from deep purple to pale, pale grey. The severe military lines of the castle with its great towers and battlements, contrasted acutely with the soft silhouette of the spreading elms in the gentle light. As they journeyed, the crimson melted into brilliant orange, paling at last when dawn came, to the deep glowing cream of the sun.

A small thicket of beech and walnut was found on their arrival, the cart covered with branches; the horse tethered. Then alone, Peter set off to seek a man he knew, a Frenchman who might sell his help. The tiny cottage was mud and stone and its small slit windows opened only towards the sea. Peter knocked, glanced anxiously around him, then waited.

Jules le Gonidec was not pleased to be woken at such an early hour. He was never pleased to receive visitors at any time, being more a recluse than the fisherman he was thought to be.

'Do you remember me, Jules,' Peter asked in Breton, his eyes squinting as the old man's lantern was held up to light his face.

Jules le Gonidec frowned, narrowed his eyes and looked again. 'The English lad, is it?' he said at length, bending sideways to peer behind Peter. 'You are alone?' he growled mistrustingly.

'I've three friends, but they are hidden in the copse.'

The old man stood listening with a cocked ear before he spoke again. A seagull wheeled obligingly above their heads, uttering its loud mournful wail, and the sea whispered onto the sand down below.

'Hidden, did you say?' he queried, going back inside his house and beckoning to Peter to do the same.

'Yes, I need your help, Jules. I cannot pay with money but a gold bracelet would fetch a good price.' He held out one of Louise's bracelets. His own money had been taken at the prison. He had nothing himself that would fetch more than the clothes on his back.

The old man took the bangle and held it close to the lantern, screwing up his eyes to examine it; feeling its weight in his hand. 'What sort of help?' he demanded, rubbing the side of his unkempt beard.

'A passage for four to Guernsey!'

'Four men who can handle a boat?' Jules asked, leaning forward with glaring eyes.

Peter shook his head. 'No, three are women, only I could help.'

'You want a lot for a measly bangle,' he

said, turning away, poking at the glowing ashes in the black firegrate and laying a small log on them hopefully.

'There might be another one like it,' Peter bargained. 'They're a good weight, I tell you. You can feel that. And you know where to sell them, a man like you always does.'

Jules grinned, showing black edged teeth; a glint came into his heavy-lidded eyes. He always knew how to get the best price, and gold was easy. 'Three women,' he considered thoughtfully. 'What sort of women?'

'A mother and her two daughters.'

'French women?'

'Yes.'

'And what might you be doing with three French women?'

Peter opened his mouth.

'Want to wed one of them do you?'

Peter sighed. It was too long a story and safer left unsaid anyway. He nodded and left it at that. He couldn't put such an untruthful declaration into words.

'Want me to drop you on a beach?'

'That would be fine.'

'Tonight?'

'If possible. We're out in the open here.'

135

He glanced at the log that Jules had put on the fire, it had caught alight. He wondered if he dare ask to bring the de Chauvelins inside. It wasn't the sort of place one liked bringing ladies; not even clean, and Jules le Gonidec stank.

'Been travelling long?' the question was asked with brisk directness.

'All night by horse and cart.'

'Who wants you?'

Peter inhaled through closed teeth. 'Some men south of St Pol de Léon,' he offered.

'Pigs, revolutionary pigs?'

Peter nodded, Le Gonidec's hatred of the sans coulotte was no secret, they interfered with his trading. The more aristocracy there were, the more buyers. He was shuffling around the room now, pushing things into drawers, then he picked up a plate and a cup, last night's supper by the look of them, and elbowed open the door at the back of the room.

'Got some ham,' he called to Peter with an impish grin. 'Go and get your women. Bring 'em inside to warm.'

Peter turned to the door gladly.

'And cut some logs whilst you're out

there,' Le Gonidec called. 'I didn't have time last night.'

Peter laughed. Sly old devil. He'd all the time in the world. Couldn't be bothered, more like. He closed the door behind him and set off at a steady jog. Twenty minutes later, and Louise, and Marrietta were kneeling by a glowing fire. Their mother sat sipping hot coffee... Outside there was a loud splitting noise, as Peter wielded the rusting axe. He was cutting enough logs to keep Jules le Gonidec well warmed for weeks.

SEVEN

The diamond necklace bought passages to England for three on *The Penelly*. She was a single masted cutter, rigged fore and aft and mounting twelve cannon. Peter had gladly accepted the suggestion that he work his passage, although the lack of food and exercise that he had experienced in the prison made his physical condition far from ideal. Louise seemed to be bearing up surprisingly well in these harsh conditions. Peter found himself watching her on the few occasions during the voyage when he saw her. How he longed to take away the sadness that was so marked on her face. He knew that the presumed death of André Renoir had affected her deeply. She had not loved him, but she knew only too well that had she accepted his offer of marriage he might still be alive. He had given his life for her and the knowledge ate away at her heart every minute of the day.

The de Chauvelins had been allowed to use the Captain's cabin. Peter had needed to bargain for even that, it being the only separate cabin below. The Captain had assumed that his French passengers would stay on deck for the voyage and should consider themselves fortunate that he allowed them on his ship at all. Peter had fought for their privacy. There were thirty men on that ship besides himself, he could not work and protect the women from all of them. He had seen the gleam that had come into the men's eyes when they had sighted Louise. He had heard their muttered appraisal of her, and had worked with sailors long enough to know that any woman was at risk in their company. In the Captain's cabin there was at least a lock on the door, and unknown to the de Chauvelins he had bought a guard for it by signing a paper on which he promised to send money to the Captain on his return home.

He approached that guarded door now, being off watch for a time and wishing to ascertain that the ladies were as comfortable as possible. The man on watch nodded in curt recognition. He had been instructed to let only the Captain and Peter into the cabin.

Peter's knock, and answer to a 'Who is

there?' from Louise, let her turn the key and welcome him into the cabin with a faint smile.

'Is there anything you need?' he enquired glancing round intently, Marrietta was still lying in the hammock which Peter had slung up between the beams for her. She looked deathly pale and coughed at intervals; her breathing was fast and laboured. He looked at Madame de Chauvelin who sat silently by her daughter's side. Her eyes were glazed as if the cares were becoming too much to bear again, the anger, the aliveness had gone. She had little stamina and little ability to find hope or comfort in the mere fact that they were still alive.

Peter laid a hand on Marrietta's forehead. It burned. Louise came close to him and touched his arm. 'We have used all of our drinking water to cool Marrietta,' she whispered. 'Is it possible that we could have more, Monsieur?'

Peter nodded. 'I'll bring you some. Has she eaten today?'

Louise shook her head. 'I think it is better that she does not. If we can have water for her, that will be enough.'

He looked down into her defeated eyes.

There had been such a brilliant light in them when he had met her at André's cottage. He glanced quickly at Madame de Chauvelin, thinking he was being watched, but her head was lowered, her eyes closed with weariness.

He brought his own eyes back to Louise and took her cold hands in his.

'It will not be long before we are at my sister's home,' he told her gently. 'Another few hours and we shall make harbour.' He pressed her hands, fighting hard against the intense desire he had to take her into his arms. 'I promised you Christmas in England, Louise. You do not think I said it lightly? There will be great celebrations. And with care and good food, Marrietta will soon get well again.' He touched her face, so cold, yet so soft, for a moment he did not move, he stood looking down into her brown eyes, remembering the words of André. 'Perhaps even you will find her desirable as a wife!'

How he had laughed, scorned away the idea, but now it seemed suddenly as if there was nothing in the world more desirable to him. Marrietta stirred, coughed a little and whispered her sister's name.

Louise turned her head, but before he released her hand, he lifted it gently to his lips. 'I will make you happy again, Louise,' he whispered. 'I promise you will laugh and walk in the sunlight with joy in your heart.'

She lifted her eyes to his and smiled, a beautiful trusting smile. 'I believe I shall, Monsieur,' she said softly. 'But my sister has need of me now.'

He let her go, glancing over her shoulder at the still sleeping Madame de Chauvelin. She jumped slightly, giving a snort and Louise covered her face quickly to hide the giggle that had almost escaped her lips.

Crossing to the door he laid his hand on the key. 'I shall bring water and anything I can find to warm you, Louise,' he told her. 'Lock the door when I am gone.' He smiled. 'And Louise, will you not call me Peter?'

A glimmer, a shine of hope flickered in her eyes now as she turned from Marrietta's side. 'Au revoir, Peter,' she said.

He listened when the door closed behind him until he heard her turn the key, then he hurried off to the galley where he obtained water, two tankards of hot grog, and an oil lamp. When the key turned and the door opened, he handed them rather disappointingly to Madame de Chauvelin, who gave him a brief 'Merci, Monsieur 'arvey, merci beaucoup.'

The wind tore at the canvas up on deck, the night sky was heavy. He hoped it would not rain before they were home. He thought of Lowarth Tek, the house that had been home since they had moved to Cornwall. The glowing fire that would be in the grate, the well laden table and the warming pan in his bed. He had set off to fight the French and succeeded only in rescuing the French from the French. The country he had thought to conquer had enough problems without the wars she had waged.

He imagined Louise sitting on the sofa by the fire in a pretty gown.

Always since they had met, she had worn the plain black of the Breton peasant with the starched white bonnet. Not that there was much starch in Louise's bonnet now; it had been too battered by wind and rain. But Louise had a dignity. Whatever she had done she had done it with elegance; climbing out of the small boat onto the beach on Guernsey, hiding in the hedgerow whilst he ran to the cottage of the Guernsey fisherman he knew. The finding of *The Penelly* so soon had been a stroke of good fortune, she had been coming in that very night to pick up a free trade cargo to smuggle back to Cornwall...

It was not an hour to dawn. The Captain had agreed to have them put ashore at the harbour from which Michael usually fished. Another half hour and they would be on land.

'Ship astern!' The cry came shrill in the darkness.

The Captain appeared, holding an eyeglass to his only remaining eye. 'She be a cutter,' he growled. 'The King, I'll wager and she'm gainin' on we. She lookes a hundred tooner.'

The cutter spread all of her canvas and Peter saw quite clearly that she was closing in. A boy was ordered to the masthead to loose the gaff-tops'l. The gap widened for a time, but soon the revenue boat was gaining again. They were well into the coast by now. Peter cursed, the last thing he wanted was to get himself and the de Chauvelins involved in a fight with the revenue men.

The deck was alive now, men climbing

the mast to trim the sails whilst others primed the cannons in readiness.

'We'll have to sink they. Cut away!' the Captain bellowed. His men needed no other word, the kegs, already slung at intervals around the boat splashed down into the waters as their anchored ropes were cut. Peter helped willingly in this well known ritual of contraband sinking. He had done it often enough before when he had sailed with Michael.

The Penelly sailed on, leaving behind her the free trade cargo to be 'fished' on another night by local fishermen, who with cross bearings made now by the Captain, and their creepers attached to long ropes would retrieve the whole cargo.

The Cutter was really gaining ground now, the keg sinking having slowed the pace of the smuggler's boat. A loud boom rent the night air as the ball fell wide of its target. The mate relayed the order to drop anchor and the canvas was lowered. Quickly, Peter searched for the Captain, his eyes scanned the swaying deck but he could not pick him out. He ran aft, then slipped down below where he found him checking the hold.

He saw Peter and grinned. 'We'll let

they smell the fish, twill keep 'em happy.'

Peter nodded, thrusting out an eager hand to help with the hatch. 'And the ladies, what about the ladies? You won't want them aboard with the revenue men here.'

'Damnation, I'd forgot they, completely forgot they.'

Peter leaned forward seeing his chance. 'If you let me have a boat I'll take them ashore myself. We're near enough now, I could make it rowing once the dawn comes.'

The Captain stamped his foot on the hatch cover, ensuring it was down firm, then he looked at Peter and frowned.

'And when do I get my boat back, and the money you promised,' he demanded.

'This very day, the money, and the boat on the first ship that makes for Boscastle. Tomorrow at least I'll wager.'

'Aye, then. Aye. Get the women on deck and I'll help 'ee down. The maid's sick. You'll need a lift with she.'

Peter wasted no time, he was already half way to the cabin. He explained rapidly and bade them get on deck with haste. Then he took off his coat, wrapped it quickly around Marrietta, then lifted her up in his arms.

Helping hands reached down to him as he climbed, the boat was already tossing in the larger ones' swell. Only moments later and he was seated with oars swinging firm in the crutches. Madame de Chauvelin sat holding Marrietta's head on her lap as her daughter lay well covered in the bottom of the boat. Louise crouched in the bows, silent and trusting. Peter pulled firmly on the oars, getting the stroke, knowing only too well the necessity for getting well out of the revenue cutter's path. Only the swish of the water and the creaking of the rowlocks touched their ears, then after a while Peter stopped rowing, laid the oars carefully along the gunwhales and sat motionless listening. The smell of the salt and seaweed filled their nostrils.

They could see little in the darkness, but some distance away a lantern glimmered as the smuggler's cutter stood patiently at anchor waiting for her pursuers to come along side. They had not to wait long, the King's boat swished fast through the water, setting up a swell that rocked the rowing boat where she stood.

Peter could smile a little now, he imagined the faces of the revenue men, defeated faces he had seen so often. The feeling of pleasure known now to the Captain as his holds were inspected freely to reveal nothing but shimmering fish.

A pale light began spreading above the horizon, heralding the dawn that was to come; silhouetting the low hills beyond the village. Peter watched the growing light with concern, soon it would spread over the dark earth and reach the bay, and they would be discovered with no hope of escape.

A shout came suddenly across from *The Penelly* but it was only the revenue officers preparing to return to their own craft. Rocked gently in the ebb and flow of the tide they watched in silence as a lantern swung down the hull into the longboat anchored below. Then the splash of oars and it swung across the lugger's stern. Soon, the revenue cutter began moving, turning into the wind, then veering southwards. Peter watched, his arms hanging wearily across his knees; his mind alive enough to know amusement that they would likely spend some time with a grappling hook, in some vain attempt to find the cargo which they knew full well had been sunk. But without the evidence, there was no way that the smuggler's cutter could be held. And she weighed anchor, hoisted her sails and headed swiftly for home.

As the dawn rose, so Peter took up the oars, swung his aching body into a monotonous rhythm, and took the small boat across the churning bay. Streaks of silver touched the crests of the rolling waves as the light of morning heralded a brand new day. On shore, lights still flickered in the windows of the fishermen's cottages and the fish cellars. It was too much to hope that this was a day when Michael would be there. He often rode to the harbour early to start work with the men and women he employed. It was seven a.m, and the sky grew lighter every minute; a pale hyacinth blue with indigo clouds. The workers would have been busy for an hour already.

As the boat glided nearer the water's edge, they heard the ripple and hiss of water on shingle. Peter boated the oars, laying them over the thwarts. When she grounded seconds later, he jumped out into ice-cold water and began the task of heaving her up onto the beach. Louise stood up tentatively, and would have jumped in beside him, but he told her to wait until he could at least help her down onto damp shingle.

149

It was slow work, helped little by the tide as the boat was well laden, and made harder by aching limbs and total fatigue. Then abruptly, the weight lightened, the boat slid more easily, grinding onto rounded pebbles. He leaned for a moment to get his breath, his body bent wearily over the gunwhale. Then he turned startled, hearing a movement beside him.

Michael stood there, his hands on the boat, his dark brows knitted as he stared at the three bedraggled women.

Peter sighed, managed a brief laugh. 'I'm back!' he said.

Michael nodded. 'Aye, I see, and the ladies?'

Peter reddened, suddenly a little embarrassed. 'Eh... Oh!... This is Madame de Chauvelin and her daughters... From Brittany,' he added.

'And have you rowed all the way from France?' Michael enquired, one eyebrow raised in question, and that glint of humour already back in his black eyes.

EIGHT

Louise laid out a gown of lime green crepe. It was decorated with white satin ribbon and she stood looking down at it with pleasure. It seemed so long ago that she had stood gazing down at her own gowns in the Château, thinking how sad she was to leave them behind. Her mother had at first insisted that she continue to wear black, but Rosalie had intervened and persuaded her that as they had so far received no news to confirm that her husband had been executed, it was surely wrong to presume so. It *was* Christmas, and Marrietta and Louise must be allowed to enjoy themselves a little after their terrifying ordeal. So new gowns had been ordered and the lime green was the first to arrive.

She sighed happily as she put it on for the first time this evening. How glad she was to see Marrietta so improved. Peter had been right; with the care and warmth and good food, she soon had colour in her cheeks again. She was still under the strict supervision of the Doctor and was not allowed out, but she would be able to enjoy the Christmas celebrations in the house.

Louise glanced out of the windows at the English countryside that she must learn to know as her own. The day had been cold, white frost had covered the lawns and hedges and only the brief, mid-day sun had melted it into green again. Now there was snow fluttering down and the sky, all afternoon had been like lead.

It was a self conscious Louise who stepped softly down the wide staircase into the wood panelled hall below. Peter was there, busy fixing red-berried holly over the dining room door. It was Christmas Eve and they had spent the afternoon decorating the large fir tree which Mansel Polruan, Michael's handyman, had brought in. It was eight days since they had arrived together on that cold, wet beach; since Michael had sent for the carriage and had them conveyed at once to the warmth and welcome of his home.

She had seen Peter every day, but since their arrival had had little opportunity to speak with him alone. His eyes had spoken to her many times, however. He turned as he heard her light footfall, and stepped down from the oak chair on which he was standing. She looked away from him to hide the flush that came to her soft cheeks and lifted the white lace fan which had hung from her waist.

'You look enchanting, Louise,' he told her, crossing the hall quickly and taking her hand to help her from the last stair.

'Thank you,' she said shyly, glancing round the hall at the greenery which decked the wide picture rail, and at the crimson candles flickering on the centre tables. Peter followed her gaze with pleasure, and saw her eyes rest for a moment on the piece of green that hung just to the left of the table. He smiled, and still holding her hand he led her beneath it.

'An English custom,' he explained, watching her large eyes grow wider with interest. 'That is mistletoe, and when standing under mistletoe, a gentleman is allowed to claim one kiss from a lady.'

Louise opened her mouth, but had no opportunity to say whatever words had come to her surprised mind. Peter bent his head and claimed his prize.

She made no move away from him when

he raised his head, but stood quite still, her lips a little apart and her brown eyes locked firmly into his blue ones. Above them their shadows danced on the ceiling, merged together as one. Then suddenly, Peter moved again; grabbed her almost roughly into his arms and kissed her as he had never kissed a woman before. When he let her go, gently, carefully, she stood breathless in front of him, eyes wide and unwavering.

'Louise, my dearest Louise!' was all he could gasp. How often had he been tempted, now at last he had done it, and he was glad.

'I believe that this was more than one kiss, n'est ce pas?' she whispered softly.

He smiled, his eyes lit bright. 'This gentleman found the first one so enchanting that he was absolutely compelled to have more,' he told her, his voice soft and deep.

The sound of Rosalie laughing came to them through the closed drawing-room door. Louise jumped a little, startled back into the reality of where they were.

'Maman will come down soon for dinner,' she exclaimed in a whisper.

Peter reached up and breaking off a tiny

sprig of mistletoe, he tucked it carefully into the pocket of his waistcoat. 'Another English custom,' he explained with a grin, 'to be prepared, then one does not miss opportunities.'

Louise turned her head away from him, and fluttered her fan gracefully. 'I believe I shall find your English customs most interesting,' she informed him as she reached the drawing-room door.

Peter, crossing the floor quickly had opened the door for her to reveal Rosalie, endeavouring to teach Michael the Gavotte in the centre of the room. They were watched amid great hilarity and laughter from Peter's younger brother Ben, and by Alice Morley who had been Nanny to Rosalie and her brothers, and whom Rosalie had been delighted to bring to Cornwall. She helped Rosalie with the running of the house and especially with their baby son.

Michael, tightlipped and radiating impatience, walked swiftly to the window when Peter and Louise entered the room.

'You shall not escape it, Michael Pendeen,' Rosalie called after him laughingly. She looked to Peter. 'Tell him he must learn it, Peter. We have been invited to a ball in January. Michael says we cannot go because he does not know the steps of such dances.' She moved her eyes to Michael; his back was to her; his eyes firmly fixed on the snow-touched garden. 'You danced perfectly well at the barn dances we had at Tom's farm. Why can you not learn the steps of more elegant dances?'

Michael swung round, his black eyes fierce with anger. 'You have forgot, Rosalie,' he threw at her bitterly. 'I was reared in a barn.' He strode briskly to the library door which led off the drawing-room, then slammed it behind him.

Rosalie stood quite stunned, her eyes closed and her brow puckered deeply. She opened her eyes and let out a deep sigh.

Peter indicated to Louise that she should sit by the fire, then he turned to Rosalie with a frown. 'Do you not consider that Michael tries hard enough already to please you?' he rebuked her.

Rosalie sat down on the sofa, her hands over her face. 'I do not wish him to go just to please me, Peter. I believe he would enjoy the ball once he was there.'

Peter moved to the window and stood where Michael had stood, his hands clasped behind him. 'I believe he would hate it, Rosalie. Truly, I believe he would hate it.'

She lifted her head thoughtfully, then rose quickly and joined Peter by the window, putting her hand on his arm. 'Then we shall not go,' she stated firmly. 'In truth I find it less and less attractive.' She turned her head to look at Louise and smiled. She had not missed the flush of Louise's cheeks when she had come into the room, nor the look that Peter had of being pleased with himself. 'But you shall go, Peter,' she announced, turning him round to face her, 'and you shall take Louise!'

Peter raised his eyebrows, he would not deny that the idea appealed to him greatly. He glanced across the room and caught Louise's eyes, delight sparkled from them. 'And a chaperon, Rosalie?' he enquired of his sister.

Rosalie waved an arm of impatience. 'Oh, do not concern yourself with that. I shall find one quite acceptable to Madame de Chauvelin.' She looked at Peter for a brief moment then she crossed the room towards the library. 'I shall tell Michael

157

that I do not wish to go after all,' she announced before opening the door and closing it softly behind her.

He was sitting at the table, a large book open in front of him and a quill held loosely in his fingers. His head rested on his free hand and she doubted that his mind was on the writing he intended. She walked over to him and laid her hands on his shoulders, saying his name in a whisper.

He rose immediately to his feet, dropping the quill carelessly onto the table as he walked away from her to the corner of the room. His eyes began scanning the shelves as if he were searching intently for some much needed book, ignoring her as if she were not there.

She swallowed hard, seeing how right Peter had been. 'Michael!' she whispered again, not moving from the spot where she stood. 'I came to tell you...that I have decided not to go to the ball anyway. It would be much better to let Peter go. He can take Louise, it will be a good opportunity for them to get to know one another.' She waited. Michael turned his head and looked at her hard but said nothing. Then he returned his gaze to the books and let his finger run slowly along the titles.

'Michael! Oh Michael! I'm sorry!' she cried, tears welling in her eyes.

He turned right round and faced her now. 'Sorry for what?' he demanded roughly. 'Sorry that you wished me to dance like a woman!' He came back towards her, his eyes still dark with anger. 'You ridiculed me, Mistress Pendeen. You made jest of me in the presence of a guest, the presence of a servant even. I know my place. I'm aware I shall never be truly worthy to be your husband. But I have done my utmost to be so.' His hand crashed down on the table in front of her, making her jump at the noise. 'I have worn the clothes I have thought you would wish me to wear. I have conceded to any whim or fancy you might have. But I will not,' he banged the table again, making the quill and book dance a jig, and the candle flicker rapidly in a haze of black smoke, 'I will not,' he repeated, 'have you scorn the place where I was born. I will never, d'you hear me? never have you laugh at me again in the presence of others.'

Rosalie stood motionless, shocked by what he was saying. She had not intended

159

scorn, she had thought little of what she said. Now she saw it through his eyes and knew that the blow she had dealt him was worse than any lash of the whip. Tears filled her eyes and for a moment she just looked up at him in a daze. Then she saw the anger melting; the light began to burn in his eyes again. He held out his arms and she needed no prompting as she flew into them and buried her face on his chest.

He lifted her chin and kissed her on the mouth. 'Were you in earnest?' he asked doubtfully. 'Will you really not mind if we do not go to this ball?'

'I was in earnest Michael. I had thought you would enjoy it, I was wrong, I see that now. And Peter will like the opportunity to take Louise.'

He nodded and sat down on the chair which he had left so abruptly. Then he pulled her down onto his knee and proceeded to kiss her with no little fervour.

'Michael!' she gasped, when she was able to take breath. 'Someone might come in!'

He grinned. 'Then let them!' he replied quite unconcerned. 'This is my house, is it not? And you are my wife. If I wish to kiss you in the library, then I shall do it, whenever I choose. Besides it is only Madame de Chauvelin who concerns you. If it were Peter, or even Alice you would not care a jot.'

She laughed. 'I believe that you do not care for Madame de Chauvelin!' she exclaimed, teasing him.

He shrugged. 'I do not mislike her, but I fear she is not what she seems.' He laid his head on one side thoughtfully. 'I'll wager if Peter starts wooing Louise in earnest, he'll find no friend in her mother.'

'You believe she will object to Peter?' she asked in amazement. 'But he saved their lives!'

'Aye, and she'll be grateful for a time; but when this cousin of hers comes in to it, mark my words, Peter will be tossed into the ditch.'

'But Louise, will she have no say in the matter? Peter said that she took control of everything during their escape. His admiration for her began with that very fact.'

Michael sighed. 'Louise will do as her "Maman" says will she not?' His face was serious now, he touched her cheek and ran his finger down to the line of her jaw. 'As you would have done, had your parents been alive. I've no illusions on that score, my love. Your father would have forbidden you to wed me.'

She kissed his forehead, then found his mouth. 'But I did wed you, Michael, and I'll never want more than I have in you.' She sat up suddenly. 'I told you that once before. Do you remember...that day when you first brought me to show me this house.'

He smiled. 'Aye, I do, but you wanted more than me this very day; you wished for a man who could dance a gavotte.'

She flushed, annoyed that he should have reminded her. 'Well, that's over now, I shan't wish it again.' She put her hand suddenly into his pocket and took out his watch. 'Good gracious!' she exclaimed jumping off his knee, and crossing quickly to the door. 'I promised to help in the kitchen fifteen minutes ago. There's so much to do for tomorrow.'

Michael laughed, stretched out his long legs, and clasped his hands behind his head. 'Are you stuffing the turkey or making mince pies?' he asked her with a wicked twinkle in his eye.

'Never you mind what I'm doing, and it's time you were entertaining our guests.'

She was quiet for a moment, listening at the door. 'It sounds as if Madame Chauvelin is in the drawing-room. You should be there, telling her what a splendid young man Peter is, what good prospects he has with you.' She turned and waved her finger at him. 'And don't forget the inheritance he has in trust when he's twenty-one.'

Michael got to his feet and took a wide sweeping bow. 'No, Mistress?' he mocked her good humouredly. 'And am I to convey to her your desires that she should join you in the kitchen to watch Peter's sister making mince pies?'

'I'm not making mince pies, they were made days ago.'

He ignored her interruption. 'In truth, I doubt Madame de Chauvelin has ever visited a kitchen in her life.' He grinned. 'I can still see her face when she was informed that we had no personal maid for her here.' He crossed to the door and dropped his hand on the knob, then he leaned down towards her and kissed her cheek. 'You are very beautiful, my love,' he told her in a whisper, 'and your face is flushed. I doubt Madame de Chauvelin will believe you have been reading books in here.' Then he opened the door before she could answer, giving her a push from behind so that she burst suddenly into the room, her cheeks pink, and her mouth open with surprise. Michael however, when the door fully opened, was nowhere to be seen.

Rosalie gathered her wits swiftly and said a polite 'Good evening!' to Madame de Chauvelin who sat erect and very composed on a red velvet chair, her face quite as white as her high starched cap and her eyes fixed into the affectation of an amazed stare, as her hostess leapt with such indignity into view.

'I will see Hannah about dinner,' Rosalie told them, tripping lightly to the hall door and making a mental note that Michael would pay for that one. In the hall she heard a persistent cry upstairs and knew that her son was awake. Then Alice Morley's voice came down to her, talking to the baby and then, singing gently. Rosalie sighed. How glad she was to have Alice here! There had been so many things she had had to learn. She, who had been used to a house full of servants had become Mistress of a house with only a man and his wife, and a maid coming in from the village each day. Alice had been invaluable, teaching her the things about housekeeping that she had hardly known existed. But Alice was getting old, she would not be with them for ever and Rosalie dreaded the day when she would have to run the house alone...

Dinner was well over when the sound of singing voices penetrated through the stout oak of the front door. Even Madame de Chauvelin showed some pleasure as the carol singers were ushered into the hall by Michael and bidden to warm themselves by the kitchen fire. The snow came thickly now, layer on layer to blanket the cold earth, sparkling as it fell in the light of the brass lamp which shone outside the front door.

The small group stamped the snow off their boots gladly and brushed the thick flakes from their hats and shoulders. They looked cold; inadequately dressed for such a wintry walk. They crowded eagerly around the roaring kitchen fire, where they were handed mugs of leek and chicken broth, and requested to help themselves to the tray of mince pies and tarts which were placed at their disposal.

When they were warmed and had eaten

well, they were shown into the parlour where they stood with glowing cheeks, and sang more carols for the delight of their hosts. Marrietta was so excited that she could hardly contain her pleasure. She and Louise joined in with the French words of many of the carols; their mother allowed her hand to tap out the rhythm on her black-gowned knee.

Peter had hardly taken his eyes off Louise for the whole evening. When the carollers had finished he leaned over and whispered something into Rosalie's ear. Rosalie smiled and nodded her head.

Then 'Louise,' she said speaking in French, 'Will you and Marrietta not sing for us? Mayhap there is a carol which we do not know.'

Louise glanced to her mother, obviously needing approval before she answered. Peter scowled, and Michael exchanged a knowing look with his wife.

Madame de Chauvelin smiled briefly and inclined her head. 'An excellent idea, Mistress Pendeen,' she acknowledged, indicating to Louise that she should go over to the pianoforte which stood by the window.

The visiting carollers muttered amongst

themselves until William Hooper, a son of the Camelford clockmaker and seemingly spokesman for the group, explained that they really ought to get on their way as they had a good walk ahead of them. The men shook hands with Rosalie and Michael, and the ladies dropped a quick curtsey before they filed into the hall to begin their long trek back to town. Rosalie doubted that it was a real surprise to them to find small packages awaiting them in the hall, and half a sovereign each in their hand. Michael was well known for his generosity. His own good fortune had not made him forget the poverty of the peasants of his native Cornwall. The workers at the fish cellars had been given a feast on the day before and had returned to their homes equally well laden. Not that Michael was wealthy, there were times when he had to count the pennies with great care. Fishing was an erratic business and there had been more than once in the last few months when the thought of returning to smuggling had more than just crossed his mind. The seining for pilchards which was done in the harbour was almost at the end of its season. In January these fish would be hardly seen at all as they kept too close to the sea bed.

Louise sang beautifully, accompanying herself at the pianoforte with surprising talent. Peter was quite overcome, and applauded so loudly at the end that Rosalie had to dig him in the ribs to make him stop. The rest of the evening passed amiably enough, but a loud knock on the door shortly before ten o'clock, heralded an unexpected visitor. He was ushered quickly into the dining room by Mansel Polruan, where Michael joined him immediately. Peter watched with a frown, until he, too, was summoned.

'Jack Carne has just come in from Roscoff,' Michael explained as Peter came in.

Peter saw immediately what the visit was about. 'Seigneur de Chauvelin?' he asked eagerly. 'You have news of him?'

The man nodded. 'Taked a deal of findin' did 'e, we thought they'd moved 'e to another prison. But t'weren't so. When we set sail 'e was still alive.'

Peter sighed, thanked him, then went on quickly. 'And André Renoir? Did you find anything about the schoolmaster?'

The man shook his head, scratching it, cap in hand. 'Nay, Master Peter, not a word. Clamped up on 'e like a clam they 'ad.'

Peter's eyes dropped with sadness, yet it was no more than he had expected. There was little chance that André was alive, but there had always been a hope. If he had found the slightest sign he would have risked trying to get him back to England.

'I passed on the name,' Jack Carne was saying. 'Telled they others I did. Might find something about 'e yet, let 'ee know if I do.'

Peter smiled. 'Yes...thank you. And thank you again for coming tonight. Have you walked all the way?'

'Aye. Baint all of we got 'orses you knows!'

Peter nodded. Michael had kept silent. Now he reached in his pocket and took out a guinea. 'For your trouble, Jack. And take a horse if you can ride. I'll tell Mansel to saddle one for you.'

'Don't need no saddle, Michael. Never used one of they, but a pony'd make things real easy this night. I'll send 'e back straight away. You tell Mansel t'leave the door loose, 'e'll find 'is own way 'ome.'

Michael nodded, offered him a warm

drink before he left, but Jack Carne had been at sea and wanted to get home to his own family this Christmas Eve.

'Well,' Michael sighed, as he closed the door behind him. 'Shall we inform Madame de Chauvelin that her husband is still alive? She says so little on the subject that I have a notion that it is of little importance to her either way.'

Peter frowned. 'I would I could tell Louise that André was alive,' he said passionately.

'She at least will be glad about her father,' Michael reminded him gently. 'Come, let's get it over with, then I'm for bed. 'Tis a busy day we have tomorrow. I've you in mind for taking the carriage to the farm for my mother and Tom's family. If this snow keeps on coming you'll likely have to dig your way there.'

Peter's blue eyes lit with humour. 'Then I shall take Ben, he's better with a spade than I. What time are we expected?'

Michael shrugged. ' 'Tis for Christmas dinner and the rest they are invited.' A glint of devilment flickered in his black eyes. ' 'Twould be best if you started at dawn. 'Twould give you time for a good morning's digging.'

Peter waved a contemptuous hand. 'I'm driving to the farm, Michael, not London town! And the snow'll likely turn to slush in the night.'

Michael shook his head doubtfully, but made no further comment. He crossed to the drawing-room door and went in.

Rosalie had retired to the nursery to feed her son; Madame de Chauvelin and her daughters were waiting to bid their host 'Good Night'.

'I have good news, Madame,' Michael announced. 'Your husband is still in prison, but he's alive. I've word just come from France.'

Madame de Chauvelin did no more than just nod her head slowly and murmur, 'Merci.'

Louise was more obviously delighted, then she looked at Peter and he knew the question that was in her wide eyes.

He shook his head sadly. 'Nothing Louise, nothing about André,' he told her quietly. Then he went to the window and pulled back the drapes so that he could look out over the snow.

A few moments later, a light touch on his arm made him turn. Louise stood beside him. Her mother had taken Marrietta up

171

to bed and Peter had not heard her. 'Bon Nuit.' Louise had remained for a moment, pleading that she wished to ask more of Monsieur Pendeen. But it was to Peter she moved as soon as her mother had left.

'Rien?' she whispered.

He shook his head seeing the heartbreak in her eyes. 'We are still endeavouring to find news. But I am sure he is dead, Louise. It is better that you accept it. And he would not want you to mourn him.'

There was a wetness in her eyes now. 'He was so very good to me Peter; and to die, because I asked his help,' she murmured almost to herself.

'He was glad that it was he from whom you sought help. He told me that, Louise. His only care was for me to get you safely to England.'

Michael coughed, reminding them that he was still there. Then he opened the library door and said in a very loud voice.

'I must look that book out for Tom before he comes tomorrow.' Then he vanished from view, leaving the door slightly ajar in case he needed to make a swift re-entry if Madame de Chauvelin returned.

172

Peter smiled, knowing Michael well enough to see clearly his intention. He took Louise's hand and brushed it with his lips.

'Do not grieve for André,' he told her gently. 'Tomorrow is Christmas Day. A day of gladness. I wish so much to make you happy, and I feel that André would wish it, too.'

She looked pale, the sudden reminder of their escape from France brought vividly to her mind.

Peter felt in his waistcoat and pulled out the mistletoe. It brought the expected smile to her lips. She glanced nervously towards the library door, afraid that Michael would re-appear.

Peter gave a brief laugh. 'Do not concern yourself with Michael,' he assured her in a lowered voice. 'One day I shall tell you about Rosalie and Michael, but you must not tell your mother, she would be too shocked.'

Louise raised her brows, but made no comment.

'Rosalie had neither mother nor father to keep an eye on her. And the things she got up to!'

A flicker of amusement crossed Louise's

face. 'Ah, oui,' she agreed softly. 'And her brothers? Is it not true that they ran away to sea?'

Peter looked distinctly uncomfortable, not wanting to be reminded of what he now considered a childish prank. 'Oh!' he said curtly. 'You know about that, do you. Did Rosalie tell you?'

She nodded. 'Oui, and she did tell me also how it was that she met her Michael.'

'I see.' Peter was greatly disappointed by this revelation.

Louise touched his hand. 'You are not angry that I know these things?' she asked.

He leaned down towards her. 'No, I'm not angry. I would have preferred that you did not yet know all the stupid things I did when I was a child.'

'You were little younger than I,' she reminded him shyly. 'Do you then consider me a child?'

'No, of course I don't, to me you're a very beautiful woman.' His eyes searched her face; his heart was thumping. 'And I do believe I am in love with you, Louise.' He did not wait for an answer, he bent his head and kissed the palm of her hand. The mistletoe fell unheeded to the floor as his arms closed around her.

When at last he released her, she bent to pick up the mistletoe which by now was well trodden underfoot. 'I do not believe we need this English custom,' she whispered.

He tightened his arms around her; his lips found hers and lingered. How long he would have stood there holding her in his arms he did not know, but Michael whistling softly, 'God rest you merry gentlemen' reached his ears and he knew it was time that Louise was following her mother up to bed.

'We'll talk again tomorrow,' he whispered into her ear. 'Good night, my darling Louise.' Then he let her go slowly throwing her a last kiss with his hand as she took the candle he gave her and melted into the shadows on the stair.

NINE

The snow did not turn into wet slush overnight, it stayed firm and crisp. Layer upon layer it grew deeper as large white flakes floated gracefully down, covering the fields and stone hedges, icing Roughtor and the Moor like a great white cake.

Peter woke early and at once he knew it was a beautiful day. He was not usually given to poetic thoughts but as he opened the drapes he sighed at the stark beauty of Cornwall under snow.

Ben grumbled loudly at the intrusion of brightness into the room and buried his head under the covers, but Peter laughed, crossed the room to his brother's bed and dragged the covers off him with no mercy for the coldness of the morning. Ben tried to grab them back again, but Peter kept them out of reach.

'Come on, up!' he ordered. 'We've some digging to do by the view from the window.'

Ben stared at him with alarm. 'Digging!'

he cried.

'Yes, digging the road out to get the carriage to the farm for Michael's mother.'

Ben groaned, crawled off the bed and went to poke at the ashes in the firegrate. 'We'll not bother with a fire up here,' Peter announced beginning to dress. 'We'll go straight down to breakfast.'

Ben stared at Peter with amazement. What had happened to this big brother of his who always lay in bed until Mansel had lit the fire...

Michael was already at breakfast when Peter put his head around the door. 'Could you not sleep?' he enquired with a grin.

Peter ignored his humour and set-to with the bacon that was keeping warm on the hob. Ben arrived down a few minutes later, looking cold and miserable.

'Hey! 'tis Christmas Day. Why the long face, Ben?' Michael cried when he saw him.

'I'm cold!' Ben grumbled. 'And Peter says we've to dig out the road.'

Michael frowned, then, pouring out tea for Ben, he handed it to him with a short laugh. 'I shall go with Peter,' he told him kindly. 'You shall stay here and entertain Marrietta.'

The relief that had momentarily crossed Ben's face vanished in a flash.

'Oh, no?' he groaned. 'I haven't to stay with that silly girl have I?' Giving up his room to her had been bad enough.

Michael roared with laughter. 'You do not know your good fortune. I'm certain Peter would be only too glad to stay with Louise.'

'That's different, and besides, Louise doesn't giggle all day and want to play silly games. I don't mind Louise.'

The door opened suddenly and Rosalie came in carrying her son. 'You will be home in time for us to ride to Church, Michael?'

Peter called 'Good Morning' to her and lifted a cheerful arm. Rosalie smiled but did not answer.

Michael nodded slowly. 'This is why I wish to go early, but if Tom has the cows milked in good time, he will likely start on the road.'

Rosalie frowned doubtfully. 'But will we get the carriage to Lanteglos, Michael. Will not that road be blocked as well?'

Michael smiled. 'If we reach the farm then we are part way to the church, are we not. I'll wager the church wardens

178

will clear the road as far as the bend. 'Tis only likely to be troublesome in the hollows anyway. A pair of good horses will take that carriage through.' He glanced at his brother-in-law. 'Now, Peter, are you ready?'

Peter was still eating and appeared not to have heard. He sat with a far-away look on his face staring at a blank wall.

Rosalie sat down in a chair by the fire and held her baby so that he could dance on her knee. 'Are you not well, Peter,' she asked him, watching his face with concern.

Michael laughed and leaned down to whisper in Rosalie's ear. ' 'Tis starlight in his eyes,' he said in a loud enough voice for Peter to hear it and blush.

'Michael!' Rosalie exclaimed. 'Do not tease him so.' She watched her son, pushing up on his chubby legs and lowered her voice so only Michael could hear. 'There have been times,' she reminded him, 'when you, too, have had starlight in your eyes.'

He knelt down on one knee on the floor beside her and took his son's tiny hand in his. 'Aye,' he conceded quietly, 'and it still goes with me every step I take. I only wish I could believe that Peter's will stay as bright as has mine.'

'Sh,' she warned him in a whisper. 'Peter will hear. The basket's ready for you to take, Michael. I put it on the table in the hall. Take care how you go, the wind gets stronger with the hour.'

He nodded and went to the door. Peter rose to his feet without speaking and followed him. The basket was heavy, full of food and small presents for those in the cottages that were scattered around. As Peter knew well, the journey they were taking was more than just fetching Michael's mother and brother's family. It was also to deliver what would most likely be Christmas dinner to any home within two miles distance of the house they were just leaving.

The horses pulled well. As Michael had said, it was only in the hollows where the snow had drifted that they needed to wield the long handled Cornish shovels they had brought. By nine o'clock they had visited six small cottages and given more pleasure to their occupants than even they could have known.

When they came within sight of the farm, they met Tom, busy with his own shovel, preparing the way for them. The return journey was no easier because another bridle path was taken; more packages were delivered and more peasant families knew the joy of receiving Christmas fare. They arrived home safely by ten-thirty and began preparing immediately for another journey to the church at Lanteglos. Only the ladies rode in the carriage. The men went on horseback which for Peter, Michael and Tom was much more to their liking. The church was full despite the weather, despite the fact that many had walked: most had come a fair distance as only a handful of cottages were near to the church.

Once back at the house there were presents for everybody. Peter was on tenterhooks, waiting for Louise to open the one from him. He had bought her a book of English poetry (knowing full well that Madame de Chauvelin could not read it) and a china bedroom clock, decorated with hand painted roses.

'To Peter from Louise,' Rosalie was reading, and he looked up with surprise, not expecting anything.

The small parcel seemed reluctant to be opened as he fumbled with it, quite red in the face, and sure that every eye was on him. Only two eyes watched, two large brown eyes, the others were too occupied with their own presents. At last the paper came off. Inside there was a brightly coloured kerchief which Louise had purchased from the shop in Camelford with money which Michael had put at her disposal. Inside this, and wrapped in a small leaf from the mistletoe bough was a silver ring. He slipped it into his pocket before anyone else noticed and read the neatly written note on the slip of paper.

'Whatever becomes of me,' she had written, 'I will always love you.'

He lifted his head at once, finding Louise's eyes. His own were shadowed by the uncertain meaning of those brief words.

Whatever becomes of me! What did she mean? The ring he recognised as one from her own finger. It was of little value, but all she had left of the jewels she had brought. To Peter, it meant everything. Quickly, he rose to his feet, placing the note in the pocket with the ring. He must find out at once whatever it was that had made her think it necessary to write that note.

A parcel was thrust into his arms by an excited Ben. 'That's from Michael and Rosalie,' he told him.

Peter thanked him mechanically and carried the parcel over to the pianoforte. Louise was busy opening packages and he couldn't see which one. He began to take the wrapping off his own and admired the richly embroidered waistcoat inside with little of the exuberance he would usually have shown. Rosalie came to him eagerly seeking his approval.

'Do you like it, Peter. I saw it in Launceston and knew I had to have it for you.'

'It is beautiful, Rosalie,' he told her, 'do tell Louise to come to look at it.'

Rosalie moved away, saying nothing more and within seconds Louise was at his side.

'Thank you, Peter,' she said rather formally. 'Thank you for the book. I shall read it when I am alone. And the clock, it is very beautiful.'

'Oh, you have them,' he said unconcernedly, the matter no longer of importance to him. 'Louise,' his face was tortured by disorganised thoughts. 'Louise,' he said again quietly, 'what do you mean, whatever becomes of you? What do you mean?'

She looked down at her hands and fiddled with the finger where the ring

183

had been, all colour draining from her cheeks.

'Maman has had a letter,' she said almost inaudibly. 'It has come by the...' she hesitated, unsure of the word.

'By the mail coach?' he offered.

She nodded. 'It is from Dartmouth, from the cousin of my mother.'

'But Michael did not say there was a letter!' he exclaimed with surprise.

'I do not believe he knows this. Your...Mr Polruan, he brought it from the town yesterday.'

'And what does it say, this letter that has upset you so?' he demanded bluntly.

'When I say it is from my mother's cousin, this is not correct, she is dead, Peter, but her husband, he has written. He says we must come at once to his house, that he and his son will welcome us gladly.'

'I see, then does your mother intend to go soon, is this what concerns you? We had hoped you would stay here longer, Michael has told her she is welcome.'

'Maman says as soon as Christmas is over, we must make the arrangements.'

Peter frowned, considering the situation, then he smiled. 'But I will still come to see you. I can ride to Dartmouth; stay overnight at the Inn.'

Her eyes told him immediately that his assumption was wrong. 'Why not?' he demanded, his voice rather louder than he intended.

She was looking down at the floor again, he put a gentle finger under her chin but she would not lift her head. Then he saw tears on her cheek, and knew that somehow he must see her alone, away from this room with its crackling packages, with its exclamations of pleasure and its watching eyes.

The parlour door opened suddenly. Betty Polruan came in to say that dinner was ready. Peter cursed under his breath as Marrietta dived unexpectedly under his arms and pushed a blue shawl under Louise's nose for her to see. She admired it dutifully without lifting her head.

'You will show it to Ben,' she said, her voice scarcely loud enough.

Marrietta bounced away. Peter held out his arm in readiness to escort Louise to the dining room.

'Mayhap you would care to take a walk after dinner, Mademoiselle,' he suggested softly. 'The path through the wood will be most handsome in the snow. And I am sure that my sister could lend you a pair of good boots.'

Louise nodded; lifted her wet eyes to his for just long enough to flash him an understanding smile.

'Maman will rest after dinner,' she told him. 'A walk in the snow will be most pleasurable.'

Dinner was unending, for so it seemed to Peter, being polite to everybody was more than he could tolerate. Twice he snapped at Tom for nothing at all. When the ladies withdrew he excused himself and going straight up to his room, he put on his greatcoat before stepping out into the snow. He knew it would be ages before Louise would be able to join him, so he just carried on walking, his deep footprints leaving clear evidence of the way he had gone. When an hour had passed, and all he had done was torment his mind with a host of possibilities, he retraced his steps and settled himself down on a low branch of one of the oaks. A place, he considered, where he could see anyone leaving the house, yet was out of view of any of the windows.

Louise came at last, wrapped tightly in a

wool cloak of Rosalie's, her hands hidden in a thick fur handwarmer. She did not see him at first but she followed the prints until he called her name and she joined him in the shelter of the thick, gnarled trunk.

He took her in his arms straightaway and heard her sigh his name as she laid her head on his shoulder and buried her face in the warmth of his coat. He let out a long deep breath of relief; the worst, the unbelievable of the possibilities was unfounded. She wanted him as much as he did her. Then whatever it was that had been thrust in their path could be removed. Like the snow, it could be brushed aside if you had the will.

He kissed her first before he spoke and she laughed because his face was so cold. The snow had stopped; even the wind had turned fickle and blew softly, sweeping the thick flakes gently away from the shiny leaves of a tall holly not a yard away.

'Now you can tell me,' he said firmly. 'Now you can tell me what it is that has troubled you so.'

She lifted her eyes and this time there were no tears. 'It is the letter,' she said bravely. 'I have not read it, but Maman says there is a son. Already he is twenty-five, and he does not have a wife,' she swallowed hard, then went on. 'Maman says that I must make myself very beautiful for him; that it is important for her, for Marrietta, and for my father that he likes me.' Her voice faltered, but he tightened his arm around her and she continued. 'She says I must make him like me so much that he will wish to marry me.' She stopped again, seeing anger kindling in his eyes, but she knew it was not for her. 'I have told Maman that it is you... She says, Oui, she has seen me smiling at you and I must not do it again.' She dropped her eyes. 'I believe she will forbid me to see you when we have left this house.'

He kissed her forehead and let his lips stay there as he spoke. 'She has not even seen this man,' he breathed, anger evident in his deep voice, 'yet she plans for you to be his wife.'

'But this is the custom, even in England. N'est-ce pas?'

'Not in my book, nor will it be in yours. I will not let it be so. You are very young Louise, yet many girls marry even younger. I believe you must meet this man; see if he pleases you. If you find you can love him...then I will not hold you to any promise to me.' It was a generous gesture and one he might regret from the bottom of his heart, but it had to be made. Louise's happiness was the most important consideration and this man could undoubtedly give her more than he. There would be other girls, though holding her as he was now it was impossible to imagine wanting anyone else.

He frowned, feeling her shudder and not knowing whether it was with cold or from the thought of marriage to a strange man. 'If you mislike this man, Louise, if you do not want him for a husband, then I shall fight for you with every breath I have in my body. Do you hear, I shall fight, with every word, with every sword, with every means I can find.'

'But Maman, she will insist!'

'And so shall I, Louise, and so shall I.' He glanced across to the house, then up at the sky. 'I fear it will snow again soon and it would be better that your cloak is not wet. You must go, ma belle Louise, but have no fear; I have fought battles with your French Navy, a battle with a French mother cannot be so very terrible.'

He released her taking a last lingering

kiss. 'Au revoir, do not forget, I love you.'

When she had left him and he had watched her cloak turn past the stables, he was less confident. He was sure enough now that he loved her, but her mother considered him unsuitable. Who was he, when the cards were laid plain on the table. He was aware now of the reason for his unreasonable behaviour towards Tom. Michael's brother, his wife Jenny and even their mother Mary Pendeen were suddenly intruders into the refined world of which he professed to belong. Michael charmed any lady with his sweeping bows, his slim height and twinkling black eyes, Madame de Chauvelin had been taken in by Michael immediately. But no-one had explained to her that he took a bath, as did Peter, on his return from the harbour every day, because even if he had only supervised a seine, or the loading of barrels, he still stank of pilchards.

Tom had undoubtedly washed well under the pump at the farm, but there was still an odour of cows about him. Even in their Sunday best, Jenny and he bore no resemblance to the kind of guests who would have graced Madame de Chauvelin's table at the château. Peter, for whom it had never before brought concern, was suddenly ashamed of the family into which his sister had married. He wished with all his might that Ben, Rosalie and he still lived at Charlesworth Hall in Nottinghamshire, with a house full of servants and a cotton mill to their name.

He began walking again, quite unaware of the thick flakes that choked the air. He walked until his hands and their fingers and his feet and their toes, were numb with cold. Then he plodded miserably back to the house, and sat gazing into the fire in his own room, staring into the flames with growing despair.

TEN

George the Third and Queen Charlotte had produced fifteen children. Thirteen of them were still living, and the Prince of Wales was already notorious for his wild behaviour and extravagant spending.

Sir Joshua Rutherford had had only one son by his French born wife Annette before she had died. His subsequent marriage to Lucille Stuart had been childless. When she too had died, five years ago, he had thought himself past marrying again at sixty-two. He must look to his son for more heirs.

George Rutherford was not the pride of his father's life. He was well named, called as he was after the Prince of Wales. His tastes were remarkably similar, although the Prince being thirty-one and six years his senior had, no doubt, more experience in acquiring both debts and women.

George had spent the previous summer at Brighton with the Prince's set, which included Maria Fitzherbert; then they had returned to London for the winter. The letter from his father that had summoned him back to Dartmouth to meet some vague cousin from France had been most inconvenient. But the letter had said, 'I insist!' and his father's 'insist' had been supported by the sudden withdrawal of his allowance from the bank. George Rutherford had come meekly, albeit bad temperedly home.

He stood now in the library, gazing out over the wooded ground, watching the River Dart trembling its sparkling way towards the sea. The snow had melted as quickly as it had come and the river was swelling with flood and tide. He could see the drive from this window, a grey strip that zig-zagged up the hill from the great, wrought-iron gates beside the gatekeeper's circular cottage.

The summons from London had it seemed been for other matters than just the arrival of his cousin. It had lately been brought to his father's attention that the gambling debts attributed to his son, now exceeded fifty thousand pounds. His father had issued an ultimatum.

'I have decided to take my guide from the King,' he had said, and George had needed

193

no explanation. It was well known that the Prince of Wales, although becoming rapidly infatuated by Lady Jersey, was in the unenviable position of having a Royal bride chosen for him. The only incentive to his accepting the situation was a promise obtained by the King that parliament would subsequently pay off his enormous debts.

'On the condition that she is a lady of my own choosing, Sir,' George Rutherford had cut in briskly.

'And of my approval, what!' his father added sternly.

He was pleasantly surprised at his son's early submission. He had expected more bother than this.

Watching now for the carriage to arrive from Cornwall, George felt exceedingly cheerful. Perhaps this girl, this cousin of his would be a ravishing beauty. It appeared she was penniless, so she would have no say in the matter whatever she thought of him. She was only seventeen his father had told him, a mere child compared with the women he usually entertained, but then she would do as she was told and that would be most convenient, especially when he took her to London. He had no intention whatever of becoming a faithful husband. A son to keep his father happy, and then he could live the life he pleased.

His mood changed suddenly when he saw the black, leather hood of the carriage, and watched it begin its steep climb. What if she were ugly? What if she stank as some ladies at court were wont to do? He would have no buxom French woman in his bed, he was too well used to prime beauties for that. His hand flew selfconsciously to his face. Had he remembered to put on his patch? He glanced briefly into the glass as he crossed the hall to join his father in the drawing-room...

Louise was nervous as she stepped from the carriage. She lifted her skirts carefully from the wet earth and followed her mother up the wide stone staircase that led to the entrance to the Hall. Marrietta walked beside her, trying hard to convey the same cool dignity that her sister managed to impart. But Marrietta's eyes darted around her, taking in only the bright livery of the footmen, and the deep crimson carpet that covered the elegant staircase which curved to the upper floor.

They were shown immediately into the drawing-room and at once Madame de

Chauvelin was the essence of diplomacy. Louise was a little behind her mother, so she did not at once see the whole of the room, nor its occupants. She dropped a delicate curtsey before the man who introduced himself as Sir Joshua Rutherford and whom her mother had recognised from a brief visit he had made to the château all of twenty years before. When Sir Joshua stepped back, his arm sweeping a wide introduction to his son and heir, Louise felt a little sick. For a split second, she hesitated before making a curtsey and smiling serenely. George Rutherford greeted her with an extravagant bow.

'Enchanté, Mademoiselle,' he murmured.

Louise glanced at her mother and saw only a self-satisfied smile on her lips. Surely even her mother could see how this man looked. The deep pox marks on his face. The white cosmetics applied to hide them and the hideous black patch at the side of his mouth put there no doubt for the same purpose. He was overweight, and his powdered wig seemed to have suffered from over-zealous attention.

Marrietta was being introduced now, but George Rutherford barely gave her a glance; his eyes were firmly fixed on Louise and she could not escape them. Tea was brought and Madame de Chauvelin made the most of the invitation to tell the story of their escape from France. She described it as if it were a play, with great drama in her voice. When she told of André's death she wept a little into her handkerchief, and Louise dry-eyed and pale, was ashamed that her own mother could use such a thing for her own purpose. Peter, it appeared from Madame de Chauvelin's account had played little part in the escape. It seemed that as he himself had escaped from a French prison he was glad of their company and the bargaining value of their jewels to assist him. Louise sat motionless, shocked and pale.

Only Marrietta, who had little knowledge of diplomacy, or the art of finding a husband, made the situation more clear. 'Do not forget, Maman, that Peter did that,' she would say, or 'Do not forget Maman that Peter did this.' And Louise blessed her heartily for her courage in seeing that the truth was told, for she was reprimanded by her mother every time she spoke. In desperation, Louise spoke in English, knowing her mother would not understand.

'What my sister says is quite true,' she said firmly. 'It was entirely due to Monsieur 'arvey that we escaped at all.' She saw her mother's scathing glance and knew that she would at least have heard Peter's name.

'Your English is most praiseworthy, my dear,' Sir Joshua told her approvingly. 'But your mother does not speak it, I understand.'

Louise smiled. 'That is so, Monsieur,' she replied, noting a triumphant glint come into George's eyes. Never had she been scrutinised so before. There was no part of her that he had not surveyed and she wished passionately that he would get up from his seat and onto his no doubt flat feet and observe the garden for a change.

'Perhaps, Monsieur, we could be shown to our rooms,' she requested meekly, returning to French. 'My mother is I think, a little weary from the journey. She would be glad of a rest.'

Sir Joshua sprang, or more precisely tried to spring to his feet. 'Mais Oui,' he exclaimed. 'How remiss of me to allow you to wait so long, when you must indeed all be worn out. By gad!' He pulled the cord that hung by the fireplace, and, when the footman appeared, he requested that the housekeeper be sent for to show the ladies to their rooms.

Louise departed gladly, heaving a thankful sigh as the door closed behind her. The sigh would have been of despair had she heard the words that followed her polite 'Au revoir!'

Sir Joshua rubbed his hands together and thumped his son hard on the shoulder. 'Well, George?' he enquired. 'Will she do, will she do you for a wife?'

George, not usually enamoured to being thumped by anyone, grinned with pure delight. 'Aye, by Jove, she'll do. She'll more than do—she's perfect!'

'Lovely girl, I'll grant you that, reminds me of your mother though 'tis hardly surprising I suppose. Can't say I care for the mother much. But confound it! You're not marrying her. We'll pay her off somewhere out of the way with the little one. Give her a house and a few servants.'

'And the father? Do we do anything for him?' his son enquired doubtfully.

Sir Joshua shook his head. 'Not long to live, I'll wager. Not worth the trouble. Leave him where he is, can't give us any trouble there can he?'

George laughed, then he laughed again, increasing the volume with each ripple of his flabby countenance. 'By Jove, we've something here you don't find often. Not a sign of paste on her face, and I'll wager not a stay on her body, and she's nigh on perfect without 'em.' He crossed to pull the bell cord. 'Bring me a brandy,' he demanded heartily when the footman appeared. 'And—No, confound it! A bottle of champagne.'

His father laughed. 'Quite certain she'll have you?' he bated his son with a devilish twinkle in his eye.

'Aye, aye, she'll have me. I'll have her in church before March month.'

ELEVEN

Peter threw himself into work when Louise had gone. Only the day after she had left there was a cry of 'Hevva! Hevva!' from the Huer's House on the top of the cliff, whilst Peter was down at the harbour with Michael. It told them immediately that a large shoal of pilchards had been sighted. Such a cry was hardly expected so late in the season, but within minutes the seining boats were being heaved down into the water. Speed was imperative, the shoal could be worth thousands of pounds, and Michael could ill afford to lose it. Narrow streets became suddenly alive with people; the men heading straight for the quay, the women for the fish cellars where they prepared to receive the catch. It was, much to Peter's amusement, considered ill luck for women to be on the quay during seining.

He called to Michael now as he set off down the shingle beach. 'I'll take the seine!' Then he waded into the water towards the

201

largest of the boats, clambered in and took the tiller. Six men already manned the oars, and smaller boats grouped around ready to follow. At first they stayed close to the beach, watching Michael who stood on the shore with cloth covered bushes which he would use to signal.

In the distance, only a slight rippling of the water showed the position of the oncoming pilchards. As the rippling moved nearer, Peter waited, tense and expectant for the signal from Michael to shoot.

Suddenly it came, the men pulled hard on their oars, and Peter steered the seine boat in a wide semi-circle around the teeming shoal, dropping the vertical net as they went, forming a barrier from the surface of the sea to its bed, preventing the pilchards from escaping out to sea. At the same time, Jacob Trewhella shot the thwart net, and the men in the lurker boats began beating the water and shouting to frighten the fish, discouraging them from escaping between the two nets. When the nets were safely tacked together, Peter sighed with satisfaction, as did his companions, who boated their oars whilst he signalled Michael on the shore.

Slowly, the nets were warped in, heaved

nearer the shore and into calmer waters. Now began the long arduous task of tucking the seine, lifting the pilchards out of the water in baskets that were then emptied into the dipper boats to be taken ashore for curing in Michael's cellars. The dark waters enclosed in the nets flashed silver, sparkling like a thousand diamonds.

' 'Twill take weeks,' Michael forecast, 'before the tucking is done.' For they landed only as many a day as the cellars could handle. The workers laboured willingly in the light of lanterns until Michael sent them home, weary from work, but revelling at such a bountiful shoal, and the money they would earn to start a new year. Michael paid well, and both he and Peter toiled unceasingly beside the people they employed.

It was only when they returned home at night that Peter had time to really miss Louise. When Rosalie came running to them, and Michael took her in his arms. Then, Peter would turn away; wonder what George Rutherford thought of Louise and more important what Louise thought of him. She had not written since she left; everyday he hoped for a letter. Then he wrote to her himself, asking how she was; begging her to tell him where he now stood in her affections. But still no answer came. There had been a letter from Madame de Chauvelin to Michael, thanking him and his wife for their hospitality and enclosing a cheque from Sir Joshua to cover any expenses incurred by their stay. A brief line asked them to convey their thanks to Mr Harvey for his assistance, no mention of Louise; no mention of George Rutherford.

The seine was a good one. Michael reckoned that there would be a good five thousand hogs heads which would bring in something in the region of fifteen thousand pounds for the fish alone.

'Then there'll be the oil, say another five hundred and fifty pounds.'

Peter sat at the writing desk plying an agile quill. By the time he had finished a neat balance sheet was in evidence.

'Twelve thousand, Michael!' he announced with satisfaction. 'Twelve thousand profit if your guess is right.' He grinned and laid down his quill. 'And I'll wager you are, Michael!'

Michael nodded slowly. ' 'Tis a fair figure for this time of the season,' he said thoughtfully. He looked across at Rosalie who sat sewing by the fire. She lifted her head, and for a second their eyes met. Michael gave her only a slight nod before she smiled and looked to her brother with pleasure.

' 'Twould be fair to halve it,' Michael said solemnly. 'But mind, I could be wrong. If the weather worsens we could lose a great number, but we'll divide it, Peter, you and I.'

Peter stared with astonishment. 'But Michael! I could not take all of that. 'Tis your seine!'

'And have I not always called you a partner? Besides you've earned it, and you may have need of the money.'

Peter stared, the truth dawning with painful clarity. They thought he might marry Louise, and the money would buy a good house with plenty over. 'I'm grateful, Michael, and you Rosalie, for I'm sure you had a part in this. If the profit's as great as we make it then I will gladly take the half. But I have not earned it yet, and I fear I must confess that I wish to go away for a few days. I know 'tis reckless of me when the tucking's only half done. But I must go.' There was sadness in his voice that had been there for some time.

'You're riding to Dartmouth?' Rosalie asked, not raising her head from the gown she was making.

'Yes!' was all he said, and they knew better than to question him more.

'Then we shall talk of money when you return,' Michael said, seating himself on the sofa beside his wife. He smiled, and gave half a laugh. 'Don't concern yourself about leaving, there's plenty of hands willing to do the work. 'Tis only the weather that concerns me.' He put an arm around Rosalie and squeezed her hand. 'Are you ready, Mistress Pendeen? For if you're not then I shall retire without you.'

Rosalie laughed; folded away the cloth into her work box and let him pull her up onto her feet. 'Good night, Peter,' she said, kissing his cheek. 'Do not stay long, for it will be morning soon enough.'

When they were gone, Peter crossed to the sofa and lay back on it with a sigh. If only he knew. If only Louise would write! The decision to go to Dartmouth had come only the instant he had said it. Now he wondered at its wisdom. But at least if he saw Louise he would know how they stood. This waiting for letters that never came was driving him insane...

Suddenly there was a loud banging on the front door. Peter woke startled, finding himself still lying on the sofa and the candle almost gone. He lit another swiftly and answered the door himself as Mansel had been in bed long ago. Jenny Pendeen, Tom's young wife stood panting on the door step. Peter pulled her inside, seeing terror on her face.

' 'Tis Tom!' she gasped, still short of breath from running. 'Tell Michael, 'tis Tom.'

Peter called loudly up the stairs. 'Michael! Michael!'

'What's wrong with Tom,' he asked her, taking her arm and ushering her towards the drawing-room door. 'Is he ill?'

'No,' she cried, pulling away from him, and very near to tears. 'I cannot stay, get Michael. Tell 'e they've taken Tom fer informin'. Michael knows 'e wouldna do it.'

'Who's taken him, Jenny, tell me who?' Michael's voice came from the stairs as he ran down, his face dark with anger.

Jenny fell into his arms, exhausted by the long walk from the farm. 'The Kelenak brothers, Michael. They said we bought too many cows of late to be gettin' money just from the farm... They said 'e was seen talking to the King, and when they was raided last Tuesday at Trebarwith, they said 'twas Tom told they a cargo was due.'

Michael sat her down on the oak chair in the hall. 'Did you not tell them 'twas I gave you the money for the cows?'

She nodded, sobbing now. 'Aye, Tom telled they, but they didna believe 'e. They said 'twas likely you was informin' an' all.'

Michael lifted both arms in a gesture of exasperation and raised his eyes to the ceiling. Then he let his arms fall with a sigh. ' 'Tis most likely I'd inform on freetraders when I was wanted for it myself,' he said with scorn. Then he bent down to Jenny, his voice quieter, his anger in check. 'Where have they taken him, Jenny? Did they say where they have gone?'

She shook her head, wiping the tears away with her sleeve. 'I dinna know, Michael. I dinna know. They taked Tom.' She looked up suddenly, and grabbed at Peter's arm, for Michael had walked towards the stairs and Peter was nearer. 'They said they'd take 'e for a ride, I mind it now.'

Alice Morley came slowly down the staircase, hearing Michael shouting and wondering what was wrong. Peter saw her, and explained quickly what had happened, then added,

'Get Ben, Alice, tell him to ride to the farm and stay with Michael's mother and the baby till we come.' He looked at Michael. 'I'll saddle the horses while you take Jenny to Rosalie.'

Michael nodded his approval. 'Is your horse tethered, Jenny?' he asked.

'I didna ride, Michael, they loosed the horses before they left.'

Michael came back to her without a word, lifted her up in his arms and carried her across the hall.

'I can walk, Michael,' she protested weakly.

'You've walked far enough,' he told her firmly. 'You'll rest now, and stay here till I return. I'll find Tom, don't you fear, I'll find him and give them more than a piece of my mind.'

The night was well lit by the bright circle of moon. Peter and Michael rode a short way with Ben then they turned towards the sea as he cantered away to the Pendeen's farm. The Kelenak's remark about taking Tom for a ride had told Michael that they intended to take him bound and gagged on one of their moonlighting trips and simply leave him on French soil. Not a cheering prospect at this time of war.

The road down to Boscastle Harbour was steep, bending round as it did until the bridge crossed the little Valency River. Michael turned his horse down beside the water, then climbed a narrow path until he was fifty yards or so from a cottage. Here he dismounted and Peter followed suit, glancing around; listening acutely for any warning sound. The river trickled below them, and in the distance they heard the crashing of the sea and the intermittent rumbling of the Devil's Bellows.

'I'll take the front,' Michael whispered. 'You're armed?' he asked suddenly, and Peter nodded, bending low and creeping swiftly towards the back of the cottage.

It was a small building constructed of stone with a lean-to kitchen at the back and two bedrooms above. Quickly, he flattened himself against the granite wall. There, he froze, listening again. A sound above him made him lift his head for a second, then he screwed up his eyes, peering into the shadows, trying to determine any object within view. A tall waterbutt formed in the darkness. He moved towards it and silently checked the wooden lid for firmness. In the next second he had climbed on top and his fingers were gripping at the tiny window above him.

The roof came right down over the top third of the window. Peter clawed with his fingers trying to slide open the frame, but it would not come. Something flew suddenly past his face and clattered loud on the stones below. He held his breath; stayed motionless, pressed hard against the wall, his fingers tightening around the pistol in his belt. There was a thudding of a bolt and the door below him eased open; the yellow glare of a lantern swinging across the path where he had stood only a moment before. Had Michael heard the noise? Would he think it a signal for him to come round the house?

A shout from inside the cottage; a mumbled reply and the door slammed shut. He breathed again and turned once more to the window. If he could lift the inner frame only a little then the window would come right out of the slot. Taking care not to dislodge any more slates, he pressed his fingers hard against the narrow bars. Slowly, gradually, it moved upwards, and soon there was enough of a gap underneath to slide his pistol to wedge it up. Now it was simple, he slid both hands underneath and lifted the pane out of the wooden groove. As he did so a muffled groan came from within the room and he knew with anger that their guess had been right.

On the bed lay Tom, not only bound and gagged, but badly beaten and in need of urgent care. Once inside, one glance was enough, Peter took his knife, cut the ropes, and slipped the gag out from Tom's mouth. Then he put his mouth close to Tom's ear and whispered softly.

' 'Tis Peter, Tom, Michael's at the front. How many of them, two or three?'

Tom's eyes would not open for they were swollen. He lifted an arm just enough for Peter to feel that he held up two fingers.

Peter lit a taper from his pocket and ran the light over Tom's body, anger lining his brow. 'You cannot walk for sure,' he said in a whisper, almost to himself. 'Then we must take them. Are they armed? Did you see Tom, are they armed?'

Tom did not answer, consciousness had slipped away from him. Peter must take a chance on the weapons ahead.

The door creaked slightly when he eased it open and he hoped they would think it was Tom moving on the bed above them. A slit of a window on the landing opened to the front of the house; Peter held the lighted taper there for a second then blew it out. Immediately, he saw a flash of steel, Michael had seen the light and was reflecting the moon on his knife.

The Kelenaks were startled when Peter stood suddenly in the doorway that opened from their stairs; startled as he had meant them to be. He held the pistol firm and bade them put their hands on their heads. Then sidling to the front door which opened straight into the small room, he slid back the bolts with one hand, keeping the pistol steady in the other. Michael came in hard-eyed, bending his six foot two under the beam.

'He's upstairs, Michael. He'll need to be carried. Can you do it alone or shall you fetch help?' Peter kept his eyes firm on the two seated men as he spoke. The slightest slip and there would be a knife through his chest.

Michael flung open the door and strode quickly up the stairs without answering. A moment later and he was down again, his brother over his shoulder and his eyes ice-cold with hate.

'Get the constable, Michael,' Peter suggested. 'Get justice by the law not with your own hands.'

Michael kicked open the front door. 'You'll pay,' he breathed, glaring at the brothers with fury. 'You know as well as I, Tom'd never inform.'

'He had the money, Michael,' Charley Kelenak ventured whining, his voice slurred by whisky.

Michael scowled. 'A loan from me, a loan to increase his herd,' he shouted at them with scorn. 'Have you so little sense that even that would not be obvious to you.' He glanced at Peter. 'Bring them outside,' he said easing himself carefully through the doorway and taking Tom to his horse.

Peter moved to the other side of the room and waved the gun towards the door. 'Out!' he ordered. 'And keep your hands on your heads whilst I tie them...'

Peter rode for ten miles that night; then another ten miles home. The Kelenak brothers walked that far, moving ahead of Peter's horse, stumbling over boulders and slipping into any hole on their path. When Peter thought they had come far enough, he tied them back to back, gagging them with a single gag, and left them high on Bodmin Moor between the peaks of Roughtor and Brown Willy. It was a bitter night and the east wind lashed hard across the moor. There were heavy clouds overhead, perhaps it would snow. Peter did not care. Even if it stayed dry all night, the Kelenaks would not forget their night on the moor. If they lived to remember it.

TWELVE

The day was dry; the sky, which for many days had been heavy with rain had brightened to a pale, grey blue. A fierce breeze blew from the sea, churning the waters of the River Dart, and tossing the scores of boats that lay at anchor in Dartmouth harbour on the swelling tide.

Louise walked briskly along the cobblestones of Baynards Cove, Marrietta at her heels and George Rutherford bringing up the rear with his father. Once around the corner and sheltered a little from the wind, they slowed their pace and Louise took time to gaze into the windows of the small shops. George thrust his face over her shoulder to discover what it was that was so enthralling her in the ship's chandler's window.

'You shall have it!' he exclaimed, seeing the model of a sailing ship at which she was staring so fixedly.

'Mais non!' she gasped. 'It is too expensive, but it is so like the one which

216

brought us to England.'

'Then you shall have it,' George repeated, stepping quickly towards the shop doorway and bending his head under the beam as he vanished inside.

Louise sighed. If only he would stop giving her presents. If only he would stop paying her so many compliments. Apart from his looks she did not find him unpleasant, but he made such an effort to please her that she was already becoming tired of his attentions. Her mother had stayed at the house and Louise had merely agreed to accompany Joshua Rutherford to the bank for a change of scenery. She had not known that George was coming, thinking he was out riding as he had said he would be.

Already her mother had given her the clear instruction which she had dreaded so much. Joshua Rutherford had discreetly conveyed to Madame de Chauvelin that his son wished to marry Louise. After a short time of consideration to conceal the fact that she had planned it so herself, the lady had consented graciously. Louise's fate was sealed, only a formal proposal was needed now.

Weeks had passed since their arrival and

no word had come from Peter. She had written to him and she had been certain he would reply, but no answer came from Cornwall. She had told him with despair her opinion of George Rutherford, and of the apparent need for urgency if he, Peter, was to help her. But still no letter had come.

George appeared now, gleefully carrying a neatly wrapped parcel which he suggested politely he should carry for her. His father had excused himself immediately and had entered the nearby banking house. Louise glanced for Marrietta, and saw her a few shops away, waving her arm and entreating her sister to join her outside what appeared to be a confectionary shop.

George held out his arm to Louise, indicating only by a brief turn of his head that he wished her to take it. To his disappointment, she kept her face averted and pretended not to see. 'Marrietta wishes to purchase some bon-bons,' she announced, hurrying over to where her sister waited eagerly.

Together they went into the shop, coming out a few minutes later to find an impatient George tapping his foot. He wasn't sure about Louise at all; most of the time she was sweetness itself, receiving his attentions with such divine grace. But there were times when he could almost believe she was avoiding him. She must know the situation, that she had been promised to him in marriage a whole week ago... He smiled to himself, a woman's privilege of course, to play games a little, to pretend that she had not fallen in love with him the first moment they had met.

The pavement was crowded around them now, sailors and fishermen hurried to and fro; street traders wheeled their carts up and down entreating anyone who passed them to buy their wares. Louise had only to comment on the prettiness of some ribbons which were displayed and they were in her hand, and George's hand was on his purse.

'Good Morning!' A tall gentleman moved towards them, doffed his hat, looked Louise straight in the eye, then passed on before they could answer.

She turned quickly, stared with amazement as he walked away down the street. Immediately she moved to the nearest window and pretending to admire the wares therein, she watched in the glass as Peter's reflection continued across the cobble stones, strode into the Butterwalk and turned out of sight.

Louise paled as she stood staring into the now lifeless glass. Then he had received her letter. He had done more than write, he had come to see her. Would her mother allow him to do so?... She doubted it greatly so she must make some effort herself. She turned to the waiting George and smiled sweetly up into his blotchy face.

'You are so kind to me, George,' she sighed, in a voice that would melt a granite heart; touching his arm with an affectionate pat. 'I really would like to buy something small for you. Perhaps you would allow me to go alone.' She turned her head towards the Butterwalk and waved a delicate finger. 'Perhaps along that street there I might find a little gift. I cannot come to any harm here, surely,' she pleaded.

He smiled, catching her hand which for the first time she did not manoeuvre out of reach. 'You will not adventure further my dear,' he warned, 'there are rough characters in this town. Watch out for your reticule, hold onto it tight. Marrietta and I will await you here. I shall truly be delighted with any little thing you might wish to give me.' He was about to say that he would be particularly pleased if she would favour him with a kiss when they were alone. But he changed his mind, deciding he really should be satisfied today with this sudden act of tenderness.

Louise smiled up at him, bestowing her most enchanting smile, then she set off slowly, patiently waiting for a passing cart before following with a racing pulse, the man she had so longed to see.

Peter stood waiting between two of the outer pillars of the Butterwalk, half hidden in the shadow, anxiously watching, yet only daring to hope that she might come. When his eyes caught the blue of her cloak; saw the joy light her lovely face, it was all he could do to restrain himself from running towards her with open arms. Before she reached him, he held out his hand, took hers firmly when she offered it and bent his head to brush it briefly with his lips.

'You did not answer my letter,' he said enquiringly, still gripping her fingers in his.

'Nor you mine!' she answered indignantly.

'Then your mother has stopped them as she prevented me from seeing you at the Hall.'

221

'You came to Rutherford Hall?'

'Two days ago. She inferred you had no wish to see me.'

'You did not believe her?' she cried, a little too loudly.

He smiled. 'I doubted her truthfulness,' he conceded, glancing around at the buildings on either side of the street. 'How long can you stay?' he asked, his eyes drawn back to her face.

She pouted miserably. 'Only long enough to buy George a present.'

'Then get one quickly, I'll wait for you in there.' He released her hand and indicated a coffee house on the other side of the street.

Louise nodded, then surveyed the contents of the window beside her hopefully. It was a book shop and displayed several possibilities. She opened the door and began quickly to scan the shelves. She doubted he would read whatever she gave him, but it had to be passably suitable. 'Letters of Chivalry and Romance' by Bishop Head. She quashed that idea as soon as it was born. 'A Prayer Book of The English Church.' She glanced through it, noting the long lists of prayers and the equally numerous pages of hymns. That

222

would do, she had no longer to consider. She paid for it hurriedly and thrust the small parcel into her reticule.

Peter had ordered her a coffee when she joined him, having chosen a table well to the rear of the shop, which was both ill lit and noisy in the extreme, Louise scarcely noticed either.

'Now tell me all that has happened,' he insisted as soon as she was seated at his side.

She related the events of the past weeks, leaving nothing untold, and emphasising the fact that her presumed marriage seemed to be marked by urgency.

'Maman has talked of a wedding in one month,' she whispered, her hand on the coffee cup trembling a little.

Peter tutted in disgust, glancing around the coffee house with a look of distaste. Then he looked back to the girl by his side and took her hand firmly in his.

'Louise,' he said in barely more than a whisper. 'This is a most terrible place to ask you, and I would give anything to have it otherwise, but I must know for sure. If I come to see your mother, if I can persuade her, will you marry me? I cannot give you half the things that George Rutherford can, but my income will not be a pauper's.'

There were tears in her eyes, and she almost dropped the cup, but a warm smile overwhelmed her beautiful face.

'I would marry you this very minute if I could, Peter,' she replied. 'Could it ever be possible that Maman would agree?'

'I'll try that first,' he told her. 'If not then I will think of something.'

'You do not wish to fight my country again?' she asked doubtfully.

He laughed. 'No, I've had enough of war, and France has enough problems with the revolution without making war as well.' He pressed her hand. 'I must see you again, and soon. But now it is time you were taking George his present.' He leaned towards her. 'Tomorrow, can you come down to the river? There is a boathouse, and a path from the Hall. I will come by boat and we can row up the river for an hour if you can get away?'

She nodded, laughing a little with pleasure. 'I will come; at two o'clock I will come.' She rose quickly to her feet, then hesitated, a look of alarm flitting across her face. 'He is there,' she whispered. 'He is seeking me.' She looked at Peter with dismay. 'What shall I do if he makes the proposal? What shall I say?'

Peter, standing beside her indicated quickly that he wished to pay the bill. 'You will tell him you need time to consider,' he told her firmly. 'He will think this quite in order.' Then turning her round to face the back of the shop, he pushed her gently through the door into the kitchen beyond. When the proprietor moved to advise him he was taking the wrong door, Peter merely thrust half a sovereign in the man's hand, and guided Louise out through the back entry and into the side street.

'He will think more of the gift if you took time to choose it,' he comforted her. 'Just walk up behind him and infer that you have been in one of the shops all the time.' He glanced around looking down the street towards the dried out mill pond. Then his eyes found hers again. 'Tomorrow. Two o'clock by the river. Au revoir. Have courage, we shall win this battle, Louise.'

George was standing still, a most peculiar expression on his face. He was beginning to be angry, yet not quite sure whether he should be alarmed. If Louise appeared suddenly, which she undoubtedly would do, then the last impression he must give was one of anger. So he stood, fingering his lace cuffs, with half a smile and half a scowl, curving his lips. Marrietta had been too talkative and in the end he had told her to be quiet. His father had not yet returned and Louise was nowhere to be seen.

Someone touched his shoulder and he moved distastefully to the side.

'Why, Louise!' he exclaimed seeing her suddenly by his elbow. 'I had grown concerned for you.'

She smiled and held out the package. 'It took so long to decide,' she lied coyly.

He smiled and sighed at his own reflection in the window glass. 'Then I shall keep it until we are alone,' he announced. 'After luncheon, we shall take a walk in the garden together, and you shall show me what you have bought.'

Louise hid her dismay with difficulty. Out of the corner of her eye, she saw Peter watching further down the street. How she wished he would come over to her and take her away this very minute.

'By Gad, what! You ready, George?' Sir Joshua strode confidently towards them, doffing his hat to a neighbour and touching it again as he reached Louise. 'To the carriage, what?' he announced, as he had

226

received no answer from his son.

George was too busy revelling in the prospect of an hour alone in the garden with Louise. At last he had melted that cold French heart and he intended to make the most of it...

That George had suggested walking in the garden was in itself rather surprising. February weather was hardly the best to choose, but then it was that or nothing and George was becoming tired of trying to contrive a meeting alone with Louise. If her mother was not present, then her wretched sister was always hanging around, and it seemed that Louise encouraged her.

George dressed carefully for the afternoon. He had chosen black velvet breeches and white silk stockings. His fine, ruffled shirt was almost hidden by the gold silk waistcoat which was embroidered in silver and scarlet. He stood admiring himself for some time in the full length glass before he decided on the coat. Still, unsure, he crossed to the window. The sun was brilliant, sparkling on the river and striking the wet bark of the bare trees so that they shone. Cold! he decided... Nevertheless! He sighed, and turned to the large wardrobe which covered one wall of his dressing room. He took out the scarlet, and the black and laid them on a chair. Scarlet, definitely the scarlet! he thought.

He put it on and began fastening the buttons. The glass threw back a colourful picture, but it showed him at once that if the coat were fastened, then the waistcoat would be hid; all that beautiful embroidery would be wasted. He undid the coat, glancing out of the window again. Perchance just this once he could bear a little discomfiture. It was after all a special occasion. Had he not gone to such trouble to see that everything was right. The summerhouse had been thoroughly cleaned and polished. That had been a sheer stroke of genius, remembering the summerhouse. The perfect place to take Louise, where they would be out of view of the house and out of that damned cold wind.

Marrietta, too, had been taken care of, although she did not know it yet. Barnes had been instructed to come into the drawing-room at precisely two o'clock, and tell her there was a surprise for her in the Boudoir. His mother had called it that, the little sitting room which both of Sir Joshua's wives had been able to call their own. It had been absolutely brilliant of him to remember his grandmother's collection of dolls. They would keep Marrietta occupied for hours. And when she did appear she would have no notion where Louise and he had gone.

His father, he knew, had an appointment with the steward. Madame de Chauvelin always rested in the afternoon. Not a thing could get in his way. By two thirty at the latest, he would have Louise in his arms and show her just a shadow of what a passionate man he was. The idea of actually desiring his wife was rather breathtakingly new to him. For the moment, he had quite forgotten Julia and his promise to fly back to her as soon as the wretched business with his father had been concluded. The ladies, he had so reluctantly left in London seemed positively drab beside this delicate French lily, who had so fortuitously descended upon his home. George Rutherford was quite beside himself with excitement.

Louise's wardrobe was rather more modest. Having only begun it anew with the aid of Rosalie she still had very few gowns. A dressmaker had been employed and work begun on new clothes for all of the de Chauvelin ladies, but today, Louise chose to wear the lime green crepe which she had been wearing when Peter had first kissed her under the mistletoe bough.

Dinner was a nightmare for Louise. Constantly she was aware of George's eyes. Bulging black eyes that smiled at her every time her own met his as if there were some great secret between them. Louise had given Marrietta firm instructions that on no account was she to leave her side for the rest of the day. When the ladies in the drawing-room were joined by the gentlemen, George paid little attention to Louise at all. His attentions were centred entirely on her mother. Louise was greatly relieved, he had undoubtedly forgotten his suggestion, that they take a walk in the garden, and forgotten also, it seemed, the gift she had bought him.

George's French was by no means perfect and Madame de Chauvelin had the habit of correcting him which irritated him immensely, particularly as the only reason he had to use it was because she spoke no English. 'The sun rides brightly in the sky, Madame,' he said, waving his arm towards the window, trying unsuccessfully to sound poetical.

Madame de Chauvelin inclined her head graciously as she was wont to do when it was too much trouble to speak.

' 'Twould be such a pity to miss the song of the birds,' he went on. Sir Joshua lifted a quizzical eyebrow at his son's sudden verbosity. George bowed slightly, not letting his purpose necessitate too much physical effort. 'Your daughter, Madame, for whom you know I have the greatest admiration has done me the honour of agreeing to let me show her the gardens. I trust Madame, that you will have no objection?'

Madame de Chauvelin lifted her heavy lids with marked interest.

George smiled and bowed his head.

'Then I am sure you will both enjoy the exercise, Monsieur George,' she purred with satisfaction.

George turned his eyes to Louise and smiled. What a little minx she was, that false look of dismay that she had so quickly put on her face. He lifted his coat tails and sat down contentedly to wait until two o'clock.

Madame de Chauvelin rose gracefully to

her feet rather earlier than was her custom. 'Come, Marrietta,' she commanded curtly. 'I shall go to my room. I have something to show you so you may as well accompany me now.'

The gentlemen had risen and stood to attention until the door closed behind their guests. Then Sir Joshua took out his watch and sighed.

'Well, time I was leaving, what! Have to see my steward, you know. Damned nuisance, but has to be done. Can't trust 'em to do it right on their own.'

He bowed to Louise, then scrutinised George with a flicker of amusement. 'Taking her into the garden, are you? Show her the flowers in that glass place.' He rang for the footman.

George wasted no time. 'And my coat, Richmond, the scarlet one, if you please. And Mademoiselle would like her cloak. Oh and tell Barnes that our little arrangement won't be needed, will you?'

Mademoiselle de Chauvelin sat in complete, utter silence, trepidation pounding in her breast and numbing her brain.

Then she remembered what Peter had said. All she had to do was to ask for time. The reason for this elaborate walk in the garden was as clear as spring water. George Rutherford was going to ask her to be his wife.

THIRTEEN

Rowing was not one of Peter's favourite
pastimes, he had, however, done it enough
times, ferrying kegs and oilskins of tea from
the smuggler's boats to the waiting men
on the beach. The River Dart was much
smoother than the Atlantic, although, tidal
as it was at this point, it could still be
rough in bad weather. The water today
was being chopped mildly by a light south
westerly wind, but the boat skimmed fairly
easily from the harbour and Peter headed
it upstream in the direction of Stoke
Gabrielle.

A pale sun burst through the clouds
as he reached the landing board which
belonged to the Rutherfords; he took it as a
good omen. Rowing past the boathouse, he
lifted one oar for a moment, pulling gently
on the other to turn the craft before letting
it slip noiselessly amongst a mass of trailing
weeds near the opposite bank. From here,
he could see the landing stage, but was less
likely to be observed himself.

The wait would be long; he had come half an hour early to allow for any hitches but there had been none. His visit to Dartmouth had been delayed for several days by the attack on Tom. Michael had needed to see that his brother's farm was well looked after until he was well again, so Peter had insisted on staying to supervise the tucking of the pilchards until Michael was free. A good man had been found to run the farm for a while and Michael had been adamant that Peter could now leave for Dartmouth.

Neither Michael nor Rosalie knew what had been said between Louise and Peter, but they had sensed that he was worried and the only cure for that was for him to see her again. Tom had been still confined to bed when Peter had left. A broken arm would take weeks to heal, but the rest of him was improving every day with good care from Jenny. The Kelenak brothers had, it seemed, been found after a discreet word from Peter and had retired to bed with, at the very least, a severe chill.

Peter waited for an hour, but Louise did not come. He began to be concerned. What reason could there be for her not keeping her promise? Her mother of course; George

Rutherford. There were a score of reasons why she had not come. He waited another fifteen minutes before rowing carefully across the river where he had tied up the boat to a nearby tree.

The land which sloped up from the river was well-wooded, enabling him to slip from tree to tree, keeping well hidden; stopping to listen for footfalls every few minutes. He had no particular plan in mind; he would play it as it came. The ground was muddy; at times his feet slipped on steep slopes but he climbed on until he reached the more conventionally landscaped gardens of The Hall. Glancing around, he saw not even a sign of a gardener. There was an Italian garden just ahead of him, and he crossed the paved areas quickly, hiding under a low arch for a moment to survey the lawns ahead.

A large wooden summerhouse stood between him and The Hall. He thought it a good point to aim for as it would shield him well from the large mullioned windows which looked out over the lawns. Bending low, he ran briskly, diving at once under the steps of the verandah whilst he listened again.

A man's voice came to him. It was quite near and he heard a laugh. Listening, motionless, his eyes darted around him searching for a way to The Hall.

'Come here!' He heard the man's voice again—then a woman's giggling—then footsteps running, echoing on wood above him—then silence.

'Come here I say, you little vixen!' The man spoke again.

The woman's reply was not clear, she made some sound of objection, then a loud cry of 'No!'

Peter waited no longer, he leapt quickly up the steps and straightened his body until he could just see through the glass. A youngish man was inside with his back to the window. Peter saw at once that he held a girl in his arms and she struggled intermittently as he forced his kisses on her. That it was Louise, he had no doubt, although he could not see her face, nor recognise the gown and cloak she wore. He dragged open the door and stood there wild with anger.

'Unhand her at once!' he shouted.

A startled George Rutherford let go of the lady so quickly that she fell to the floor. Peter saw immediately that it was not Louise at all but a serving maid, one no doubt employed at The Hall. He stood for a moment unsure what to do.

George Rutherford had in the meantime collected his senses, he stepped forward waving an accusing arm. 'Who are you, Sir? And what do you mean by entering my summerhouse in such a manner? And for that matter, what are you doing in my gardens?'

Peter saw the plastered face; the black patch. He glanced at the girl still cowering on the floor. 'Is this gentleman offending you, Mistress?' he asked politely.

She looked up at her master for a brief second, then she laughed and got hurriedly to her feet, straightening her frock which was now visibly awry. 'Why of course, 'e baint, I likes it, don't I, Master George?'

George looked decidedly uncomfortable, having been caught out by a complete stranger whose importance he had no way of determining. Perhaps his father had sent this man to find him, though it hardly seemed likely.

Peter did not wait to be asked to identify himself again, he turned abruptly, closed the door behind him and strode determinedly across the lawns towards The Hall.

George's, 'I say, my good fellow!' fell on deaf ears and Peter rang the doorbell when he reached it with angered zeal.

Madame de Chauvelin received him in the Boudoir. She had at first declined to see him, but he had sent his most humble apologies and the message that what he had to say to her was of the greatest importance. She was not at all pleased to be disturbed during her rest period and least of all by Peter Harvey.

'You have something of importance to say to me,' she enquired hardly raising her eyes to his face, and using her customary French.

'Indeed I have, Madame. And I do apologise for disturbing you, but I wish to ask the whereabouts of your daughter?'

'Marrietta?' she exclaimed with casual perverseness.

'I believe you know I meant Louise, Madame.'

'Why, she is in her room of course. Where else would she be?'

'Then may I ask your permission to see her?'

She laughed, quite definitely she laughed,

239

but the humour in it was as dry as stale bread. 'Certainly not,' she exclaimed as if it were the most preposterous suggestion in the world. 'Perhaps there is something you should know, Monsieur 'arvey. Monsieur George Rutherford has made Louise an offer of marriage. One which she will no doubt accept when she has spent the appropriate time considering it.'

So Louise had been right, and she had done as he had suggested. But why had she not come to meet him?

'Then there is something which perhaps you should know Madame. George Rutherford is at this moment in the summer-house.' He saw her eyelids flutter. 'With one of the maids.'

She leaned slowly back into the chair and regarded him coolly. 'And am I to be concerned with this?' she asked him bluntly.

'They are...' he hesitated, unsure of the best way to express it in French, 'in a very compromising position. I am sure you would not wish your daughter to marry a man who proposes to her on one day and then makes love to one of the maids on the next.'

She ignored his remark, totally ignored

240

it. 'I have the highest regard for Monsieur George,' she told him. 'He will make an excellent husband for Louise.'

Peter stood motionless, words escaped him. He stared at her with absolute horror. 'Then I must tell you that I have reason to believe that your daughter would prefer to marry me,' he told her, unable to conceal the truth any longer.

'And this is your reason for bringing such frivolous tales to me,' she purred sarcastically.

'I would humbly suggest Madame, that it is George Rutherford's behaviour which is frivolous,' he retorted, swallowing hard. A stone wall would be easier to penetrate. 'I would like your permission to pay my respects to your daughter, Madame. And if she so wishes it, that I may make addresses to her regarding marriage.' She said nothing, so he went on, 'I am not, I admit, in the financial position of Mr Rutherford, but my prospects are excellent, I believe, Madame, that I could make Louise happy, and this, I am sure, is utmost in your consideration.'

Madame de Chauvelin rose slowly to her feet and crossed to pull the bell cord. 'What is happiness, Monsieur 'arvey? Do you really believe I would ever consider you as a husband for my elder daughter? I would sooner she married Sir Joshua himself.' She turned back to look at him, a sneering smile on her lips.

The door opened, and a recently acquired French-speaking maid came in for her instructions.

'Monsieur 'arvey wishes to leave,' Madame de Chauvelin announced coldly. 'And perhaps, you will see to the carpet. Monsieur 'arvey seems to have been walking in the river by the look of the mud on his boots.'

Peter turned, swept out of the room in disgust. If he was to marry Louise, then it certainly would not be with the consent of her detestable mother...

It was almost dark before he returned to the Castle Inn where he was staying in Dartmouth. He had rowed farther upstream for hours before he had turned for home; mulling things over and over in his mind, until his head was dizzy with confused thoughts. If only there were a clear answer. If only there were someone on his side besides his own family.

He secured the small boat to its mooring, sought out its owner and paid him for the extra time he had borrowed it. Then he stepped briskly across the stones to the New Quay and entered the Inn with a sigh. To his surprise, there was a letter awaiting him there. A chambermaid from Rutherford Hall had brought it, the landlord told him with hopeful interest. Peter thanked him, but gave the man no indication as to his connection with The Hall, before bounding up the stairs to his room. The hand was Louise's and he could not wait to open it. Throwing his hat and cloak onto the bed, he tore open the envelope.

'Mon cher Peter,' he read and he sighed a little with relief. 'Forgive me, if you please that I did not come to the river this afternoon. I believe I was a little too eager to walk in the garden and Maman suspected me. She locked me in my room. She is already so very angry with me. Yesterday, George asked me to be his wife, but I told him I would need time to consider his offer. He was not pleased. He tried very hard to persuade me and he made me let him kiss me which was horrible. Oh, Peter! I do mislike him so. Maman is so terribly angry with me. She has just been to my room and says I shall never see you again, as you have returned to Cornwall. But my Peter, I do not believe this.

'Tomorrow, in the morning, Sir Joshua is to take Marrietta and I to visit the High Sheriff of Devon, Mr John Seale, at his home Mount Boone. We shall come into Dartmouth afterwards for a short while before returning to Rutherford Hall for luncheon. I am hoping that I might see you for a few moments in the town. I shall pray tonight that this may be so.

Your Louise.'

Peter sank onto a chair with cold anger, his knuckles white with the ferocity of clenched fists. How dare he force his kisses on her! The fellow was a rake, there was no doubt, a libertine of the worst kind. There was nothing for it, there was no other way. He would have to take Louise away; take her somewhere and wed her without her mother's consent. He rose heavily to his feet, went to the door and called the landlord to bring him up some supper. Then after eating and drinking with little appetite, he sat at the small oak table into the early hours, planning what he would do on the following day.

The wind jerked cold blasts across from

the river as Peter ventured from the Inn onto the New Quay. The heavy gunmetal clouds spoke of forthcoming rain and he dreaded that the change in weather might cause the Rutherfords to alter their plans.

The carriage arrived however, and concealed as he was in the shadowed coach arch of the Inn, he watched as George Rutherford descended flamboyantly before handing down Louise. Sir Joshua completed the party; Marrietta was not with them, and neither, to Peter's relief, was Madame de Chauvelin. They had, it seemed some purchases to make. Peter could not conceive how Louise would manage to get away from the two men, and his own encounter with George Rutherford in the summerhouse meant he would be recognised, and could not simply walk past them as he had done before. He remained hidden therefore and fortunately the group moved towards him. Louise was glancing nervously around her, obviously hoping to catch sight of Peter; wondering if he had received her letter. When she was close enough, he whispered her name softly. She turned, startled, narrowing her eyes to see into the blackness and then she smiled briefly

245

with relief as she saw him standing there. He threw her a kiss as her pale cheeks flushed prettily. And then she was gone.

He followed at a distance, taking care to keep out of George's sight. At intervals, Louise looked around, satisfying herself that Peter was there. He only had to wait now, wait until she could slip away. Sir Joshua seemed destined for the bank again. George spoke to Louise, and they conversed for a few moments before he, appearing somewhat aggrieved, turned into a doorway and vanished out of sight.

Louise wasted no time, noting that Peter was watching, she stepped into a narrow passageway between two buildings and followed it through to a small courtyard. Timber framed cottages lined the open, cobbled square, but when Peter rounded the corner, he saw Louise's cloak just disappearing behind a crumbling stone wall. It was only a small space, a blind corner between a disused pighouse and the end wall of a straw-thatched cottage, but it was sufficient for the two of them to talk unobserved. It was sheltered, too, from the cutting slaps of the wind.

Peter did not speak, he just opened

his arms and she was in them at once, held firm.

'Quid pro quo, I think Sir!' A voice behind him brought back the rough courtyard, the hard grey sky, and the awareness that George Rutherford stood behind him. All at once he was glad, relieved to come face to face with him at last.

He released Louise slowly from his arms, gently, carefully, so that she had time to collect her wits and to know from the look he gave her that there was nothing to fear. Then he turned himself around, deliberately slowly, and looked his challenger squarely in the face.

'We meet again,' Peter said, a hint of mockery in his voice.

'I should have you flogged, Sir, yes flogged!' George expounded, clearly losing his temper, yet not quite sure what to do. He looked at Louise, but she was half hidden behind Peter, who still gripped her trembling hand.

Peter laid his head on one side, considering. His calmness was undoubtedly disturbing the man who stood in front of him.

'So this is how you behave Mademoiselle!'

George reproached Louise sulkily. 'I hardly need to ask the name of your companion, Mr Harvey, I presume. Your mother warned me of him, but I did not believe you would stoop to secret meetings.' His eyes gave up their search for Louise and returned to Peter with an attempted sneer. 'I should call you out, Sir,' he said with little conviction. 'Yes, that's what I should do, by Gad! Call you out.'

Peter straightened to his full six foot which allowed him to look most decidedly down on his accuser. 'And for what, may I ask?' he questioned, eyebrows raised.

George reddened; stepped back two paces. 'Why, for this!' he spluttered, waving a vague arm, 'for making advances to a lady who is promised to me in marriage!' he ejaculated, already amazed that Peter had offered no apology.

Peter squeezed Louise's hand and pulled her forward to his side. 'Are you promised in marriage to this man?' he asked confidently.

Louise looked down at the ground unable to meet George's accusing eyes. 'I have made no promise,' she whispered. Then suddenly, she lifted her head proudly. 'And I will make none. I can never marry you, Monsieur Rutherford!'

'So you have not been as successful as you would have me believe, what!' Sir Joshua loomed suddenly around the corner, glaring at his dumbfounded son. He saw Peter for the first time and raised his brows in surprise.

'Good day to you Sir, and who may I ask do I have the pleasure of addressing?'

Louise stepped forward before Peter could answer.

'C'est Monsieur 'arvey,' she told him eagerly. 'Monsieur Peter 'arvey who brought us from France.'

Sir Joshua smiled. 'Then we are indeed indebted to you, Sir,' he exclaimed extending a hand which Peter took and shook firmly. 'Now!' Sir Joshua continued. 'What's all this about, m'dear? And what the devil are we doing in this confounded yard? Could hardly believe my ears, by Gad. Mademoiselle Louise saying she does not wish to marry my son. Can this possibly be true?'

All eyes turned to Louise.

'C'est vrai, Sir Joshua,' she said with a slight shiver.

'Then you must have a reason. Has he offended you? Has he bungled this too?'

he demanded angrily.

Louise drew back confused, a little afraid, then she remembered that Peter was still at her side. 'Mais non, Monsieur,' she cried. 'But if you please, I wish to marry Monsieur 'arvey.'

Sir Joshua was clearly taken aback by this statement knowing nothing of the earlier conversation and only discovering the group after seeing his son turn into the alley and wondering where the deuce he was bound. 'But your mother has expressed the wish for a marriage between George and you. She has given me to understand that you were delighted by the idea.'

George said nothing. He was wishing he had chosen a better place for such a confrontation. Unlike Peter and Louise he was not sheltered from the wind and it was beginning to rain in large spots.

'Then my mother is mistaken,' Louise responded quickly.

Sir Joshua forced a smile. He could see easily the attraction that this young man held for her. He was better looking than George by far. And all that gallantry, rescuing her from France. He felt a pang of envy for the father of this young man; if George had only half his courage. 'I fear, Mademoiselle that you will be required to do as your mother wishes,' he said, almost kindly. 'It is not the custom for young ladies to choose their own husbands, and...' he broke off seeing a gem of immediate value. 'And your father, Mademoiselle. Would he too not insist on this marriage, were he here?'

Peter took the bait as Sir Joshua knew he would.

'And if the lady's father objected to this union, then would you think it wrong?'

Sir Joshua smiled, bending his head slightly in acknowledgement. 'Indeed I would, Sir. Indeed I would. But how is it likely that we can obtain the opinion of Monsieur Jacques de Chauvelin, confined as he still is to a French prison.'

Peter glanced at George Rutherford; saw his brow lined deeply with confusion. Then he looked at Louise; saw only despair in her eyes and remembered his promise when they were on the homeward bound ship to make her happy.

'Then I shall go to France,' he announced simply. 'If it is at all possible then I shall obtain a letter from Monsieur de

Chauvelin with his opinion on the matter. I trust Sir, you will allow me the time,' he said addressing Sir Joshua. 'One month from today should be sufficient...' Sir Joshua nodded his agreement willingly.

'Then good-day to you, Sir, I shall make preparations at once.' He turned to Louise; taking her hand, he bent his head and brushed it lightly with his lips. 'Au revoir, Mademoiselle. I will return.'

Then he was gone, striding across the courtyard and turning down through the passageway with a purposeful step.

George looked at his father with dismay. But Sir Joshua smiled, took him a little aside and lowering his voice, he said, 'Do you believe it possible he could survive French soil twice,' he asked with a slight twist of humour on his mouth. 'Don't concern yourself with yon fellow. That's the last you'll ever hear of him I'll wager.'

George grinned. 'And shall we allow him the time?' he asked.

'But of course, Louise would never forgive you if we did not. But you can fix the wedding now. A month from today.' Then he turned and walked in Peter's footsteps across the yard. He might smile that he had successfully solved a problem for his son, but there was a little sadness in his heart to have sent such an estimable young man to his death. And all for the love of a lady.

FOURTEEN

Rosalie listened, tilted her head to one side and smiled. She could hear a woodpecker tapping its beak on the reddish bark of the wild cherry above her. She glanced upwards and saw the bird, high on the trunk. The white flowers that would soon dominate the garden with their delicate beauty were still in bud.

Something darted by her feet, and she looked down just in time to see a grey squirrel hurrying towards a nearby oak before scurrying up into its sturdy branches. A bright sun threw golden light across the garden. The sky was white with cloud, which, marked with dashes of bright blue, moved slowly towards the East. February was almost over. March month it seemed might only come in like a gazelle.

She crossed the lawn by the slate stepping stones and bent to look at her son Matthew, easing back the warm coverlets just a little to see the chubby tight-eyed face. Another month and he would be one year old; another month and spring would be truly here.

A horseman came riding hard down the lane; she turned from the perambulator and watched the gateway expectantly. Michael swung his horse into the drive and dismounted quickly, almost before his horse had halted.

'Michael!' Rosalie called, hurrying over the short tufted lawns of winter.

He saw her, smiled, and came striding across with open arms. The black eyes shone as he swung her round, but there was something hard about the line of his brow. Rosalie lifted her face to his with anxiety when he had placed her safely on the granite path.

'Something's amiss, Michael!' she challenged him, knowing his habit of bearing any problems on his own shoulders. He laughed, took her hand and began walking slowly across the stepping stones. 'I ride home early,' he began, 'to be with my wife and all she can think of is that something is wrong.'

She stopped walking and pulled his hand so that he turned back to face her. 'What is it, Michael?' she insisted. 'Please don't treat me like a child.'

He bent his head and kissed her cheek. 'Peter's back for one thing. He'll be here for tea,' he offered brightly. 'He saw Louise.'

'And the other, what's the other thing?' she demanded.

He did not answer straight away, then, 'Oh, just that Peter's decided to take a boat to fetch Louise's father,' he announced casually.

Rosalie stared. 'Fetch Louise's father!' she gasped. 'But he's in prison, in France!'

He said only, 'Aye.'

'But Michael, he cannot take a man from a French prison just like that, especially now, at war with France.'

'Nay, I'd a mind 'twas not too easy myself.' He looked down intently into her blue eyes. 'I said I would go with him, Rosalie,' he told her quietly. 'We'll do it quicker together and be back with you in no time at all.'

She did not speak; she let her eyes fall from his face until they reached the strong hands that held hers. Hands that had done almost everything a man can do. Tilled the soil, reaped the harvest, tended sheep, then worked a boat until he knew the sea so well that he was regarded highly as a Captain.

Hands that had been a smuggler's hands, now a husband's, a lover's hands. She gripped them hard and felt them tighten around hers.

'You'd best not take too long in France, Michael,' she whispered, 'or your daughter will arrive and find you away.'

'My daughter!' He lifted her head swiftly with the palm of his hand and saw the tears in her eyes. 'You're with child again?' he asked, his eyes alight.

She nodded and blinked back the tears, but he had taken out a handkerchief and wiped them away in a second.

'It might be another son,' she warned him, smiling now.

'Aye, so it might, but I'll not care. Man or maid 'twill be yours and mine. That's all that matters and I'll be back here by your side long before this one sees the light of day.'

She laid her head against his shoulder and sighed. 'When will you go, Michael?'

'On the morning tide. Peter's signing up the crew now. I could let him go alone, my love, but with the two of us, there's twice the chance and I owe him that.' He laughed suddenly, his eyes catching sight of a tiny face peeping around the side of the hood of a rocking perambulator. ' 'Twould seem our son has had enough of the air, Rosalie. Perchance like his father, he could do with a bite to eat.'

Dawn came too soon for Rosalie and the clouds were thick overhead. She had slept little knowing only too well the dangers that lay ahead for her husband and brother. The perils of the fickle sea were nought compared to the return for Peter to a village where he had been imprisoned, and where André Renoir had died for the sake of the same girl.

March had come in like a wild stallion, thundering across the land and sea with no care for anything in its path. Trees swayed frantically, their lighter branches snapped and tossed like straw. Peter feared that Michael might think better of taking out one of his ships on such a day, but he made not even a murmur against the journey. A heaving boat under his feet was as common to him as the still, firmness of the earth.

They set sail with the wind hard to starboard and their helmsman steering south-south-west. The seas were high, deep troughs took the boat down with a shattering thud, then up she came again on the next gigantic wave. Little canvas was needed at all, and the wind raged through the masts and rigging, whistling and moaning as it went.

Peter let his eyes stray around this boat they were taking to France. The *Cormorant* was a sturdy boat, a single masted cutter, rigged fore and aft and swift in sail. She had ridden many storms; he prayed that this one would leave her still afloat.

As the morning raged on, Michael, clad in oilskins, took the helm himself. The wind had veered northwards, easing a little but becoming colder every hour. The crew all knew that until they had rounded the Scillies and got well out into the English Channel, there would be no let-up on work. Even then it would depend on the wind.

Suddenly the *Cormorant* dropped vertically. To the starboard beam, a great wall of water, some fifteen feet high, towered above them. Peter dived for a firmer hand hold attempting to yell above the thunderous roar to the men on the forecastle. George and Luke saw the water for a brief second before it crashed heavily down onto the deck. Peter watched helplessly as the men vanished completely in a whirlpool of froth and swirling water. Then water rushed up the deck towards him, his own feet, knees and suddenly his waist were under its cold grasp. He bent his body against the thrust of the water, reaching desperately for the rope that lashed the raft to the deck.

Already in the deep, cavernous trough, the *Cormorant* listed hard to starboard. Then abruptly, she came up again, shuddered violently from stem to stern, tossing her head, shaking water from her deck and riding high on the crest of the next rolling wave.

Peter froze where he was; felt the water dragging down at his legs and the sudden coldness as his body was free again. George, soaked to the skin but still clinging precariously to the bowsprit, was assisted quickly back onto a pitching, heaving deck. Luke, slightly more fortunate, grinned up at them from a tangled mass of ropes, his hand still clenched tightly around a rope hook. The rest of the crew, found safe and amazingly cheerful, got back to work, able to joke now about the moments when they had thought the boat dead. Steadier, she rolled on, and within the next hour the gale died down slightly, but the bleak greyness of the sky was ominous. Michael talked of snow. The sea, reduced to a heavy, rolling swell was easier on the men, but soon the sky grew even darker; the light barely perceptible. Visibility was down to a hundred yards.

Peter was below deck, brewing tea when he heard a fierce clattering on the deck above. He swung himself swiftly up the companion ladder and thrust his head through the hatch to see hail stones as large as marbles, dancing a jig on the swaying timbers. Disgusted, he went below again, finding his hurriedly left tea slopped all over the table. He poured another quickly, drank it down between bites of bread and home made jam. Then he returned on deck to allow the next man a brief respite from the bitter air.

His thoughts during his own break had been of Louise and the man who sought to make her his wife. George Rutherford was not to be trusted an inch, but Peter had put faith in Sir Joshua's word. He said he would give Peter a month, and Peter had thought he meant it. That Monsieur de Chauvelin might be dead was a thought he could not allow. He had drawn a map for Michael of the prison, its surroundings, and any parts of the lanes around he could remember. Luke Trevelyan had been taken on as crew because he knew a good deal of the countryside in which they would need to work. He had lived in France before war was declared, to avoid a slight matter of a smuggling offence. Between them they had built up a good deal of useful information on the area. But first they had to reach French soil, and the weather seemed bent on preventing them.

The English Channel was little warmer, but the hail had stopped and visibility was decidedly improved.

It was with grateful hearts that they circled to come in against the tide, their mainsail flapping loosely and their bows set for the quayside of a small Guernsey port.

FIFTEEN

The air was thick was smoke, the smell of coffee and warm bodies when Michael pushed open the heavy street door. His eyes searched quickly for a vacant seat, then he moved lazily across the room and sank down at a table already occupied by two men. The one nearest to him puffed continuously at a long pipe, only removing it to take a noisy sip at his black coffee. The second man, altogether heavier in build, eyed Michael with guarded suspicion, seeking, it seemed, to place this tall, dark-haired stranger.

When the coffee shop owner's plump daughter appeared, Michael asked for coffee and rye bread, keeping his voice low in the hope that an English accent would not sound through his French. He had noted that the men around him were using French, attempting to comply with the new laws. His Celtic looks and shared ancestry with the Bretons made him more acceptable to walk amongst them, than did

263

Peter's fair hair and blue eyes. Peter, in addition, was known by many in this town. The bright moon on the night of André's death must have placed his clear-cut face deep in the memory of those pursuing men. He had attempted to blacken his hair and wore it loose, but he could not change the brightness of his eyes. At this moment he waited with Luke and his younger brother Denzil, hidden on the road to the coast, impatient for any news that Michael might glean. After their night of shelter in a Guernsey harbour, George had landed them on the French mainland before taking the *Cormorant* out to wait at sea.

Sipping his coffee, Michael listened intently. From a room at the back came the mute tones of an accordion. The hum of the conversation was punctuated at intervals by loud peals of laughter. Then unexpectedly, he caught a name, and held on to it. Citizen Kerbol. The group of men using such an address were seated at the next table. He saw at once the man whose name it was, and he heard other names which Peter had mentioned.

'Zut alors! Citizen Bellay. You have done nothing but sulk since we lost that girl. Find another one! I tell you there are plenty around as good as she. Most of them better for a shoemaker.' A titter of laughter circled the table.

Citizen Bellay scowled. 'I wanted that one,' he mumbled childishly. 'And her father, you said that Englishman would come back for her father. Well, where is he? We've kept the dog alive for nothing. Barely alive, I'll grant you. If we don't take him to the guillotine soon, he'll die without it. What do you say to that, mon ami?'

Citizen Kerbol threw him a look of sheer disgust. 'We've more important things to discuss than the de Chauvelin family,' he retorted, turning his back on his sullen companion. 'Voilà! Here's Citizen Le Braz.' He put up a hand to the man who had just entered at the door. 'Come, Mes amis. Now we can start our meeting.' He raised his hand again and shouted at the top of his voice. 'Liberté! Egalité! Fraternité!'

A loud disjointed chorus of shouts joined his. Coffee cups and cloth caps were raised in salute. Michael raised his own cup and mumbled soundless words. The fat man beside him still looked his way at intervals. He would be glad to be out in the Rue du Fil. When the group of men, whom he concluded were the committee of the local Popular Society, had left, he pushed his way unhurriedly towards the street door. Then, lifting a hand with a loud shout of 'Vive le Revolution!' he escaped into the blackness of the night. The information he had sought had come to him with surprising ease, he only hoped the rest would be as simple.

The following morning found Michael once again in the narrow streets of Châteaunoir. He bought supplies of rye bread and a little meat, then crossed Place de L'Apport, pursuing a faint sound which he had hoped to hear. It was market day; the place was full of noise. Beggars swarmed everywhere, their ragged clothes live with vermin, their gaunt sallow skinned faces set with sunken, pleading eyes. Michael dropped a sou here and there into trembling bowls, flashing them a quick smile, giving only a brief nod in acknowledgement of their grateful 'Merci, citizen.' Were it not necessary for him to remain incognito he would have gladly filled their bowls with the bountiful food which adorned the stalls around him. He ached to see such suffering for the sake of a loaf of bread and a hunk of cheese.

Displayed on basket woven trays, or heaped in barrels, were the fruit and vegetables of Breton's fields; the fish taken from La Manche by the scores of fishermen along its coast. Beside their wares the traders shouted their prices, uttering curses at intervals as they spied a child scrambling beneath the tables to retrieve some fallen apple before scraggy dogs devoured it out of reach. Ragged boys hovered suspiciously near to those whose purses seemed full. Members of the armée révolutionaire bellowed their views from every corner, making their opinions quite clear lest there be Government spies about.

Michael bought fruit and fish, then he turned the corner into Rue de la Fontaine, following the sound again. Even with such an intent purpose on his mind, he could not help but admire the great cascading fountain which dominated a small square off the street. There were, he had been told, one hundred and fifty figures carved into the whole work. He stood for a moment of sheer wonder, amazed that men who had carved this magnificent piece should have borne sons who were now intent on destroying their heritage.

The sound of metal ringing on metal thrust its way into his ears again, the regular beat of the blacksmith's hammer. He continued down the street until he smelt the odour of burning wood and saw the smoke of the blacksmith's fire.

'Good day,' Michael called when the tall, thin man who wielded the hammer looked up and saw him standing there. 'I wonder if you can help me. I am a stranger in this town on my way to Brest. My horse went lame some miles away and had to be shot. Could you tell me where I might buy another?'

Buying horses was not the wisest thing to do. Horses were expensive, and marking himself as a man with money would not help, but if Siegneur de Chauvelin was ill then some form of transport would certainly be needed. And horses would speed their escape to the coast anyway.

The blacksmith laid down the glowing metal bar that he was forging and thrust the hammer into the pocket of his leather apron. Then he instructed a young boy nearby to see that the fire was kept burning well, before coming over to Michael, a doubtful frown covering his smoke-blackened face. 'You've money for a good horse?' he asked less than politely.

Michael assured him he had.

'Then as it happens, Citizen, I have one for sale myself. If you'll wait whilst I take off my apron, I'll show her to you.' He vanished for a few moments inside his cottage.

Michael sauntered over to where the boy was busy pumping the bellows to the fire.

'Do you not go to school?' he asked casually, keeping his voice low, glancing around to see that no-one was within hearing.

The boy eyed him suspiciously but said nothing.

Michael was undeterred. 'I'd heard there was a good school in this place. I'm surprised to see a boy of your age not attending it.'

The boy laughed briefly. 'Then you heard amiss, Citizen,' he said. 'There is no school. It closed when the fool of a schoolmaster got himself mixed up with some aristocratic pigs.' He walked across the yard, came back with an armful of logs and tossed them onto the fire.

'The schoolmaster went to the guillotine, I should hope?' Michael commented, skilfully hiding the intense interest he had in the matter.

The boy cracked a scornful laugh. 'Guillotine! He wasn't worth it, they threw him in prison with old de Chauvelin.' He leaned a thin arm on the anvil for the moment. 'There was talk that the Englishman might come back to get them. He escaped with the de Chauvelin women, a right rumpus that caused.' He grinned for a moment of memory, then he sighed and turned to the bellows again. 'That was months ago. They're both half dead now anyway. And who wants a school, only those with money could go.'

So André was alive. He must get the news to Peter as soon as possible. Glad as he was to hear it, it made twice the problem. They would have André, too, to rescue now. He heard the blacksmith returning.

'My apologies, Citizen. My wife had some problem she couldn't deal with. No use at all, women. Can't do the simplest thing without help. And you, you scoundrel,' he shouted picking up a stick and throwing it at the boy. 'Idle brat! Get on with your work. There's harness to clean and more wood to cut. What do I pay you for? Standing around like a tethering post?'

Michael said nothing. He stemmed the impulse he had to take the blame himself for the boy's present inactivity, drawing attention to himself might do more harm than good. The stick had caught the boy on the side of his face, cutting the flesh enough to draw blood. He scurried away to the back of the forge, but not before flashing a look of hatred in Michael's direction.

The blacksmith was talking again, waving his arm towards a small side lane, and elaborating on the excellence of his mare, and his great sorrow at having to sell her. Michael followed somewhat thoughtfully, and finding the horse to his liking, he bargained for a while before paying the satisfied blacksmith and swinging himself easily onto her back. Then he turned her northwards from the town and rode away to give the startling news to his waiting companions...

André is alive! André is alive! The words throbbed on and on through Peter's aching head. Why had he not come back sooner? Why had he left it until the schoolmaster was so near to death? Whatever injury he had suffered at the time of his capture would be bad enough, but the months in prison with no hope of escape whatever, were enough to kill any man.

He had been so sure, so positive that André was dead. Now, to learn that the only reason he was not, was that the men from whom Peter had escaped hoped to use him as bait. A bait indeed of which he, surprisingly, had learned nothing. Were the traps they would have certainly have set still in evidence? He felt an urgency now, more compelling than the month's deadline he had been given to get the opinion of Jacques de Chauvelin. Rescuing André was the prime object and he knew with certainty that Louise would agree it was so. Much as he loved and wanted her, that fact had become secondary to this new, pressing objective.

The hurriedly written note from Louise which he had received before leaving Dartmouth was suddenly of use. It contained a list of names and addresses of people in Breton whom she might consider her friends. She had listed them in what she called order of trust. Peter had thought it unlikely that they would need such contacts, now he saw a value in them.

There might be things they would need for two sick men, neither of them likely to be fit enough to ride alone.

Michael had taken a room at the town cabaret. He had been seen around for days now and questions would be asked as to where he was staying. He had imparted the information that he was waiting to meet a friend who would shortly travel through this way. It had been accepted with no apparent concern. Luke was to join him at the cabaret at whatever moment was convenient to their plans. In the meantime, Luke was sleeping with Peter and Denzil in a derelict cottage on the outskirts of the town. Its roof sported large gaps which were ideal for watching the stars, and its broken down walls were covered with creeper, but it gave protection from the wind and enough cover from a showery sky.

'I shall try Marie first,' Peter announced as they had sat around a small fire made in a hollow of stones.

' 'Tis a risk,' Michael had warned him thoughtfully.

'Marie has not seen me before and she will at least be glad to have news of Louise,' Peter insisted.

So, here he was, ragged and bent to conceal his height, knocking on the door of the home of Louise's maid Marie, in the blackness of early evening.

The nights in Breton were still cold, but the weather at least was an improvement on the bitter winds and hail they had left in the Atlantic. Peter rubbed his hands together to warm them. The pale glimmer of a lamp had come through the closed shutters of the cottage and now he heard movement from behind the door. A bolt was pulled; the door swung open and a young, dark haired woman stood there.

Peter sighed, said 'Bon soir,' then his eye caught a movement beside her and at once a small boy thrust himself to her side, one whom Peter recognised with pulse-raising alarm. For the boy, who would know him at one glance was Paul-Michel Duval, son of the chief jailor whom he had taught to read.

Peter bent his head as if to bow in humility. 'Could you spare a little broth for a weary traveller?' he begged in a voice shaking as much with shock as with intention. The girl began to speak, but her voice was drowned by a high pitched shout.

'Allez-vous-en!' Paul-Michel shouted fervently, using the French he had learned first from Peter, 'espèce de gredin!'

Peter heard a sound of protest from the girl but he did not stay to see what was on her face. He kept his head down as he staggered along the path, unlatched the gate and vanished into the welcome night.

What the boy was doing there he had no idea, nor had he any inclination to find out. But as he walked briskly back along the winding lane to join the others, the experience told him that contact with any house was out of the question for him. In any home, at any door, he might meet someone who knew him. Perhaps even now, Paul-Michel was telling someone that he had seen the beggar at the door somewhere before. Perhaps by now he had remembered the face, and messages were buzzing through the town that the Englishman was back...

The men who patrolled the grounds of the Châteaunoir prison wore the uniform of the Garde National. They were well armed, but not as well trained as they might have been, had they have been recruited from towns nearer Paris. Michael's continued stay at the cabaret had proved invaluable. Nothing more had come of Peter's unfortunate visit to Marie's home. They thought it safe to assume that Paul-Michel Duval had not seen Peter clearly enough to recognise him. The idea of securing help in the town had been abandoned.

Luke had arrived at the cabaret on one of the four horses they had now acquired. He had been suitably pleased to find his old friend Michael La Plume awaiting him, (Michael had chosen the name with some humour, it being the French for Pen). The two had of course found need to celebrate their meeting and quite naturally there just happened to be two off duty guards from the prison already in the cabaret. One of them a Captain called Leonard Lévêque. As the wine flowed generously, so did the talk. The two Frenchmen enjoying the somewhat elevated position into which they were put by these two munificent visitors, drank well, sang well, and conversed inexhaustibly. By the time it was the hour for their return to duty, they had expounded not only their whole life histories, but also, more useful information about the prison than they would have dared had they been sober. That the landlord would remember the incident later Michael had no doubt. But by then, and with God's help, they would have André and Seigneur de Chauvelin on their way to the coast.

As Captain Lévêque made his way unsteadily out through the cabaret door, Luke took him aside, put a firm hand on his shoulder and whispered in his ear. The Captain's eyes lit up with delight.

'And what do you plan now?' Michael asked Luke softly when the men had gone.

Luke grinned. 'I told him I be concerned about his having to stand outside on such a cold night. I promised to take a walk over to the prison later and bring him half a bottle of Cognac to warm his blood.'

Michael laughed. 'Well thought, Luke, well thought. Now I suggest we retire to bed for a while. We've much work to do this night. The earlier we are well settled in our rooms, the sooner the landlord will be snoring in his.'

Luke nodded. The cabaret had emptied during the last half hour. The clutter of drinking mugs and glasses was all that was left amid the odour of stale smoke.

The candles burned low, the deep shadows they cast flickering into one with the great patches of darkness.

Michael called the landlord and he came hurrying in, his own eyes heavy with weariness.

'I'll be glad to be inside this night,' Luke said with a deep sigh. ' 'Tis a cold wind blows across the land by the rattle of those shutters. I'll trouble you for half a bottle of Cognac, if you please, landlord. I fancy a drink in my room to finish the night.'

The landlord nodded, handing down a bottle and pocketing the coins Luke offered. 'Aye, 'tis good to have a warm bed and a full stomach, there's many have neither.'

Michael glanced at Luke but made no comment on it. 'I bid you good night, landlord,' he called yawning, and ambling slowly down the stone passageway. 'I'll not be awake long this night, mon ami,' he sighed loudly, climbing the stair with one hand held firmly on the wooden rail.

More like you'll get no sleep at all, Luke thought, as he followed up the stone staircase, the Cognac held firm in his fist...

Two hours later, and Peter was walking

briskly with Denzil along the road to the town. They kept well in the shadows, halting at intervals, listening for the sound of hoofbeats. It was scarcely a twenty minute walk, and soon they were crouched together under a thick foliaged tree. Within minutes their watch was rewarded, two horsemen cantered along the lane in their direction, reining their mounts beside the same tree and joining them in the shadow.

Quickly Michael put Peter and Denzil in the picture, relating to them the information given to them so helpfully by the Garde National. Luke's coat bulged with the Cognac and his idea of promising it to the guard was greatly applauded. Watch had been kept on the guard for some days and their routine was well in the memories of the four men...

Only the wind seemed to stir as they made their way towards the revolutionary prison. Unlike the Château de Chauvelin, the Château-Noir was close to the town. The gatehouse, used as the chief jailor's house and through which Peter had made his escape, came almost onto the main street. The grounds of the Château sloped away to the rear and it was from this direction the four men approached it now.

Captain Lévêque was not in the least concerned to hear a movement behind him as he stamped his feet and blew hot air onto his aching hands. Indeed, he was very glad to hear it. He turned quickly, narrowed his eyes towards the approaching sound, then smiled as Luke's form began to take shape amongst the shadows.

'Welcome, mon ami,' he whispered eagerly.

Luke put his hand into his coat and produced the promised bottle. 'A companion for the night,' he breathed softly, allowing his victim to swallow a few mouthfuls before giving the signal to his waiting brother. There was something unpleasant about gaining a man's confidence before knocking him out. But it had to be done and his head would ache little more than if he had drunk all that Cognac. Leonard Lévêque fell like a stone from the blow that Denzil dealt him. Ten minutes later, he lay bound and gagged and dressed in Peter's clothes. Peter, on the other hand, looked well in the uniform of a Captain of the Garde National.

Denzil picked up the bottle and handed it to Peter with a grin. 'Your bait, Citizen Captain,' he reminded him as Peter set off to win another uniform for his companion.

The second man from the cabaret was tempted as easily as had been his Captain. Denzil dressed himself in the uniform and prepared for the next move. Moments later, and the man on duty at the prison's main door, was confronted by two of his fellow guards who held two men ahead of them at gunpoint.

'Garde à vous! We've come from Brest to collect two of your prisoners,' Peter told him swiftly. 'We've seen Captain Lévêque on his patrol and he told us to tell you it is in order for you to open the door.'

The man did not move, his face still portrayed some doubt.

'Hurry up, Citizen Corporal! Get the door open, if you please. The Commissaire said the transfer was urgent.'

The guard shuffled uneasily towards the door, his hand on his pocket, twitching the keys. Then he turned suddenly and faced Peter with an accusing scowl. 'No-one can leave the prison without written authority, you must know that, Citizen Captain.'

Peter sighed impatiently, looked across to Denzil with a facade of disgust. 'Then will a letter from your Chief Jailor, satisfy you? Do you think we would come without the correct papers? You must know that Citizen Duval is in Brest at this moment. We have already shown the paper to Captain Lévêque, and you are wasting our time.'

The corporal took the paper that Peter offered him and after a quick glance, he swung around to the door again, unlocked it swiftly and saluted as Peter led the way inside. The two passes written in the hand of Citizen Duval which Peter still had in his possession had proved invaluable. He had had no difficulty in forging the Chief Jailor's hand at all and he was glad now that he had bothered to do so.

'May I ask who these men are with you,' the guard enquired, now in a much more trusting mood. 'They don't wear uniform.'

'Do you think we're such fools, that we would do all the work?' Peter charged him. 'We were told those two dogs couldn't walk, so we've brought these men to carry them to the horses for us. Come on, mon ami. You've seen the authority. Get the night jailor I beg you and let us get on our way.'

The jailor on duty was sound asleep when they approached his room. 'And which two prisoners do you intend to take,' he asked, with a foul-smelling, black-toothed yawn.

Peter laughed, and Denzil joined in as if they couldn't believe the man's ignorance. 'Haven't you heard?' he asked him scornfully. 'Don't you know that the Englishman's been seen in the area. It's that pig of an aristocrat and the schoolmaster we've to take. The Chief Commissary wants them taken quickly to Brest, and you, Corporal,' he said to the open mouthed guard, 'must be ready to catch the English dog. Show us where these two are quickly, and then I'd set a trap for him, if I were in your shoes. That one is a cunning fellow, and he'll sneak up on you if you're not prepared.'

The guard made a hasty retreat to his at present unguarded door, and Peter shuddered a little to be once again in the place of his own imprisonment.

A frail figure lay huddled in the corner of the room to which they were taken. A figure which even in the yellow glow of the lamp, Peter barely recognised as André Renoir. As attempts were made to stir the sleeping figure, Peter kept in the shadow. If André were to open his eyes, he might recognise Peter and his condition would not allow him to act any part. He did not wake however, and it soon became obvious that for the present he was beyond stirring. For a moment of dread, Peter thought they were too late, but when Michael laid him over his shoulder they saw movement on his arm and a flicker of the heavy lids.

'Now the other one,' Peter growled his order at Luke. 'And remember,' he said sternly, addressing the jailor, 'no one must know they've been moved, not even your own men. And just be ready to catch that English dog when he comes.'

He nodded nervously. 'Of course, Citizen Captain, of course.'

They crossed now to another room where they found Louise's father, who although in the same pitiful situation was awake and raving mad, it seemed, by his continuous mumblings. Denzil touched his brother with the bayonet he had taken from the unconscious guard, and motioned him to lift up the French Seigneur. A task which a trembling Luke had no problem with at all, for neither prisoner weighed more than a child. They were dying, it was clear, as much from starvation, as from disease.

The remainder of the rescue was simple. Peter assured the guard at the door that they had horses and more men awaiting them on the road. Then they were passed without problems through the main gates to mount their restless horses. Free, but still on French soil, and with two men who had more will to die than they had will to fight for life...

André had not long to live. This fact had become painfully obvious as soon as they had laid him on the makeshift bed in the cottage, and had inspected his wounds. They were deep, festered and bleeding anew from the jolting of Michael's horse. Unattended sabre cuts, it appeared, and to Peter it seemed a miracle that he had lived so long.

When the wounds had been cleaned; his foul-smelling clothing changed and his body washed in water from a spring Peter held him up gently in his arms and touched a little fresh water onto his dry lips. The grey eyes opened slightly, and the mouth searched eagerly for a longed-for drink.

'You are safe now, André,' Peter told him, trickling more water into his mouth. ' 'Tis Peter, do you remember me?'

The white face was turned slowly upwards, the eyes moved to rest on the face above him, and his brow creased into a deep, questioning frown.

Peter went on, 'Louise is safe. She is in England.' He stopped for a second as André's hand moved slowly to grip his own. 'And soon you will see her. Soon you, too, will be in England. We have Louise's father.' He was about to tell André about his own love for Louise, but suddenly it seemed the wrong time, there would be chance enough when he was well. If he got well, of course! Peter called softly to Michael with urgency in his voice. 'We must get a Doctor. He needs medicines.' André was coughing, a hard rasping cough.

Michael was by his side, kneeling on the stone floor.

'Listen!' Peter whispered. 'A night on the sea like this would kill him.'

Michael nodded agreement. 'Aye, 'tis true enough. The Seigneur's in better shape. He's no wounds to contend with. He's taken a little broth already, although I doubt he knows what we say to him.'

'Is there no Doctor near the coast who could be trusted? There must be some who are not for the Revolution.'

'Aye, there's many so I've heard. But most are in fear of their lives. Many who continued to attend the gentry have gone to the guillotine.' He called Luke, who came over from the small turf fire they had lit. Sparks flew and glittered making swift little flames in the dry grasses.

Michael inclined his head towards André. 'We cannot move him again, Luke. We had not meant to bide here, I know, and I believe to conceal six men would be foolish. But André must stay and one of us with him. Peter asks for a Doctor.' He was thoughtful, biting his lip, then he went on slowly: ' 'Tis possible we might find someone to come. Have you thoughts on the matter, Luke?'

Luke was looking at André, great compassion in his eyes. 'As you say, Michael, 'twould not be wise to move he. He's ill wished to be sure. There be a man I mind some twenty miles away. He be a good man of medicine and not afeared to speak 'is mind neither. Though likely 'e's lost 'is 'ead for that by now.'

'Would you take a horse and ride for him?' Michael asked.

'Aye, I'd do that.'

'Then if Denzil and Peter take the Seigneur nearer the coast, they could signal the *Cormorant* and get him aboard. If we need to bide here longer with André, then Peter could sail her to Dartmouth well in time to claim Mademoiselle de Chauvelin.' He looked at Peter, his lips curved in a slight smile. 'You've to get him out of this madness first, I fear. He'll likely say that Louise can wed King George at the moment.' He got swiftly to his feet. 'Come with me, Luke! We'll need a better hiding place. There's part of the hedge over here near the wall that looks a likely place.' He was outside the cottage now, moving stones to the corner and cutting branches from the tall hedge. Soon Luke and he had built a well concealed shelter. The stones made a good dry floor and an oilskin well covered with branches formed a hidden roof.

' 'Tis certain the bound guards will be discovered by now. Another hour and it will be dawn,' Peter observed.

'Then we must act swiftly. Help me carry André to this place we've made. Then you and Denzil take the Frenchman to the boat. You'll be well away from here by dawn. I doubt even the soldiers will seek us hard till the daylight's here.'

'And I'm to ride for the Doctor, Michael?' Luke asked.

'Aye, and take care, and when you return eye this stone. If the point is to the west then there's soldiers about. If it faces east then there's none I know of.'

Luke nodded, filling his water bottle at the spring and was soon riding north east away from them. Peter and Denzil, too, were soon mounted. The Seigneur seated firmly in front of Peter as they rode at a canter towards the sea. There was a bed awaiting them in a small harbour and an arranged hour to signal the *Cormorant*. Their plans were well rewarded and before dawn on the following day they were enlightening George as to the situation, glad to be aboard, but concerned still for the three men still on French soil...

Luke had returned alone. The Doctor, already aware that he was being well watched, had refused with some reluctance to accompany him. He had, however, provided Luke with an assortment of medicines and instructions for their use. André was improving; of this there was no doubt. But it could take a week or more before his wounds were healed enough for the swift ride to the sea. Michael knew the risk he was taking, remaining so near the town, but he had to take a chance that his pursuers would assume they had all gone straight to the coast. One search of the cottage had already been made whilst Luke was away. Michael had sat beside André in their false-hedge hiding place, his knife drawn ready and his pulse at a race. But the soldiers had gone, finding only the ashes of the fire which could have been left by any one of the scores of beggars who roamed the lanes around.

It was sixteen days now since their departure from Camelford. André was stronger, taking food, lucid in speech and his wounds bled less often and needed less care. The medicines the Doctor had sent were doing their work and Michael and Luke decided it was time to make a move. Luke was to ride ahead to send the signal to the *Cormorant*, which having sailed to Penzance and landed Seigneur de Chauvelin safely in the care of George's sister, had returned to her vigil a few miles off the Breton coast.

The day on which Luke left was bright, the sun now much warmer and the wind melted into a soft breeze. The warmth brought out butterflies, and the blossom on the hedge, and it brought out a peasant family to sow their crop.

The field beside the cottage had already been ploughed, and it stood in ridges from end to end. A group of women and children arrived first, each carrying a wooden tool with which they began to harrow the ground. Later their men folk arrived, seed bags strapped to their backs. Today it seemed the whole family had turned out to take advantage of the warm weather.

Michael, doomed to spend the whole day hidden in the hedge, seethed with annoyance that today he could not lift André out into the sun as he had done on the day before. He and André had got on well during their enforced companionship; Michael had been able to tell André the details of Louise's voyage and stay in England. When André heard that Peter intended to marry Louise, he laughed; said it was just what he had hoped for, then slept content knowing that all he had suffered had at least been fruitful.

Luke would return by mid-day. Michael only hoped that he would have the caution to ride past the open field gate before riding up to the cottage with such obvious intent. Mid-day came, and went, Luke did not come. The group in the field stopped for rest, inconsiderately they decided to use the cottage wall to rest their backs. Michael and André sat in silence in their fly ridden shelter. Their mouths grew dryer as their water bottles emptied and the peasants talked of the wine they were drinking. André, able to see the humour in the situation, lay patiently, uncomplaining. The mere action of wafting away a fly, a cough or a sneeze might create sound and movement which would most certainly have been investigated in a wide, thick foliaged hedge.

It was almost dusk before the weary family shouldered their tools, closed the gate behind them, and took back to the town a small compass which the youngest had found on the floor of the empty cottage. A compass which had undoubtedly fallen from Michael's pocket as he warmed food on the evening before.

SIXTEEN

Peter had not stayed in England as Michael had suggested. Feeling that he could not happily go to Louise with André and Michael still in France, he had returned on the *Cormorant,* determined to first ensure their safety. The arrangement had been that the boat should sail close inshore at a specified point on every third night. Tonight was one of those nights and all eyes scanned the shore in the darkness.

' 'Tis there! To the west beyond that outcrop of rocks,' shouted George from the forecastle.

Peter joined him swiftly. 'Aye, 'tis clear now.' He was silent whilst they read the signal. 'Tomorrow night,' he translated the flashing beam, an overwhelming feeling of gladness and relief flowing through his body. 'They are ready to be taken aboard,' he sighed. There had been the fear at the back of his mind that something would go wrong. That he would not return in time to claim Louise. By the time her father had been safely installed on English soil, he had fortunately regained his sanity. When the situation had been explained to him, and he had learned that his whole family were safe, mainly due to Peter's efforts, he had not hesitated in giving his approval for Peter's marriage to Louise. In Peter's possession now was a written confirmation of that fact, signed in the presence of a man of the church.

A day and half a night waiting seemed unending. Peter was impatient to have Michael aboard again, and to know how André fared. The Channel was kind, her seas flowing in calm, gentle billows, and the wind right for a swift return to the English coast. As the arranged hour trickled towards them, they prepared to come alongside. An hour later, the signal had not come. Two hours; three, still the shore was black with no glimmering light to bring them in. Peter paced the deck, stormy faced and quick of temper.

'We'm to come again tomorrow night,' George reminded him gently. 'You know well enough 'tis only a small thing can stop 'ee showing a light.'

Peter nodded. He was being unreasonable and he knew it. When the silver light of dawn touched the water to the east, Peter cursed it. There would be another day of waiting now.

Darkness came again and only the mainsail was set, loose on the mast. The hours crawled by; still no light. Peter sought out George and asked him to take the cutter in.

'A score of reasons,' George reminded him again.

Peter waved a contemptuous hand. 'And one of them could be no light to show. What if they have lost their lamp? A thousand reasons more like, and half of them could use my help.'

George, seeing no use in arguing, gave the order to sail in closer and prepare to lower a boat. There was light rain now, dampening the air and blowing horizontally from the coast. Peter went below deck to fetch his already packed bag. A short trip with Denzil at the oars and he was back in France again, back in this country where he had learned so much of love and hate.

On shore, he found no sign of the three men, so walking to the harbour where he had spent the night with Louise's father, he visited the same house. There, he learned that Luke had been in for a meal two nights ago and had told them that he and Michael were to bring a much improved André down to the coast on the next night. Then what had gone wrong? Why had Luke not done as he said?

Peter took the lane back to the derelict cottage, and Châteaunoir. When he and Denzil had brought Louise's father down this lane they had turned their mounts into a wild patch of gorse covered moorland with a stream running through. As he found the same place now, he was relieved to find the horses still grazing there. With the aid of a pale moon and food from his bag, he succeeded in catching one for his own use. A few hours hard ride and he reached the cottage barely minutes before dawn. The place seemed deserted. His signal was not answered by Michael and a search of the hideout revealed little worth note.

It was as he was returning to the gateway that he stumbled and almost fell. Something lay in his path and as the faint light spanned the sky, he saw it was a man.

'Michael!' he cried, heedless of the need for caution. Then 'André!'

As the light spread from tree to tree,

from hedge to hedge and down to the muddy earth, he saw a face, a white still face with open, staring eyes. And with anger, with tearing anguish in his heart, he saw that André Renoir was truly very dead.

His clothing was covered with blood and the wound that had given it was fresh and deep. His hand clutched at the small wooden cross at his throat. That Michael must be near, Peter was sure. Glad now of the growing light, he searched frantically, tossing aside branches, beating down tall grasses and bramble with his bare hands. When he thought there was nothing, nothing at all, he saw blood on the ground, dried and hard in the soil, but as he reached it, a trail met his searching eye, one leading away from the road. It led him over the field, across a stile and into another. The possibility that Michael had escaped but was injured spurred his whole body onwards. Then abruptly the trail ended and hope was dashed. Had they caught him here and taken him back to the town?

It was the only clue he could find, the only direction he could take. He searched for another hour, crossing from field to field then he looked to the sky and he turned his face southwards towards the town to which he seemed doomed to return.

For two days he roamed the outskirts of Châteaunoir, going into the streets only after dark, playing the beggar to anyone who might pass and getting kicked and abused for his trouble. On the first day, there was a Pardon, and Peter was a little surprised that these pilgrimages to the tombs of Saints were still allowed. He concluded however that there was such a profusion of them held in Breton that great difficulty would be found in stopping them. It had most likely been thought better to allow the peasants to continue to remember their Saints in peace. The procession was all too obviously sparse in menfolk, the new calendar allowed them no time off work for feasting. Slowly, they moved towards the hillside where Peter was hidden. He observed the solemnity of their faces. The Pardons had, he thought always seemed to stress the melancholy of the people of Breton, and he wondered how they reconciled support for the revolution with this so deeply religious ceremony.

The pilgrimage, he discovered, was to

a statue, half hidden from view, by not only a growth of ivy, but also by its natural concealment in the rocky hillside. Slowly the procession filed past the statue, crossing themselves and mumbling prayers as they moved a little away. The young girls sat primly on boulders whilst the few young men present challenged each other to a wrestling bout, or, breaking off branches and sharpening them with their knives, then competed in pole jumping whilst their elders watched.

Eventually as the afternoon came to its end with lively dancing to simple harmonious rhythm, Peter sighed with relief as they began to break up into groups and make their way home. They sang as they walked, until the echo of their ballads lingered no more over the broom and gorse, and the stars began flickering in the slate blue sky.

Peter followed at a distance, awaiting the darkness before he made his way towards the cabaret. With its drink and free talking he knew this was the place to hear news, but its candles flamed brightly and his face was too well known to too many. Resignedly, he feigned drunkenness in the lane outside, listening; then suddenly, he heard his name whispered, and an old man hobbled up to him and slapped him briskly on the shoulder.

'Luke!' he breathed, hardly believing his eyes, as the familiar face showed through the dirt and wild hair.

'Come away!' Luke bade him, setting off down the street at a pace hardly in keeping with his age of the disguise.

'You know about André?' he asked warily when they were well out of earshot and hidden in shadow.

Peter nodded sadly. 'Aye, I found him. But where's Michael? And what happened to you?'

'Where's Michael, that's the question? But I can tell 'ee, 'e's not yere. I've crawled these streets for nights and only this day I had the word that 'e escaped those murderous dogs. I found that Marie, caught she alone after hours of waiting and her told me 'twas a compass they found. They came to harrow and sow and they found Michael's compass on the floor. When I got back from sending light to the boat, there be men around and watchers all night. Michael thought it safe to move when the light had gone, but the sabres flew; caught André as you see'd.'

'Then we must find him, somewhere between here and the coast,' Peter cried. Hidden, walking, crawling or dying even, Michael was there...

They searched for days, riding every lane they could find. Walking every path, climbing fences and hedges, scouring derelict buildings and keeping watch on those inhabited dwellings that were away from village or town. The days became weeks. They returned to the shore to give the news to the crew and Denzil joined them on land again. But still no Michael; still no answer to the gulls call that had been his signal for so long.

It was four weeks and a day since they had first sailed, but Peter hardly noticed the time. He thought of Louise. He thought of George Rutherford and his heart was sick with misery. But he had to find Michael, dead or alive, he had to take him back to Rosalie before his own happiness could be considered.

Day after day, they traced the same weary miles. A cottage here and a small hovel there. They questioned peasants where they dared, and they looked through lamp lit windows when the shutters were open to see. There had been rain for many days; the chances of finding Michael alive grew less each hour.

It was raining hard as they trod a narrow track and they were surprised to see a man sitting on the stile ahead of them, quite unperturbed, it seemed, by the soaking downpour.

He said 'Good day,' as Denzil reached the stile, looking hard into his face. Luke nodded a greeting, climbed over and passed on. Then Peter came trudging with little heart and the man stared hard into his face, put a hand on his arm and said softly, 'Michael's alive. I'm to tell the man with the blue eyes that he knew you'd come.'

He was lying on a bed of straw, drinking goat's milk from a cup when they came into the small, woodcutter's hut. And all three men had tears in their eyes, hardly able to contain their joy.

'André saved my life,' he told them sadly. 'He must have seen the flash of steel before I, because he threw himself in front of me as he shouted.' He looked down at the lifeless arm by his side. ' 'Twas another blade caught me hard. I became so weak with loss of blood that I could scarcely crawl. This good man found me and took me home.' He smiled, raised himself a little on the bed. 'How does Louise fare, Peter. I'll wager she was glad to see you.'

Peter turned away, a cold vice gripping his heart. 'I do not know, Michael. I have not seen her. I believe it probable she is wed to George Rutherford by now.'

Michael stared at him with dismay. 'You stayed to find me first?' he said hoarsely. 'At the cost of your own love.'

Peter whispered: 'I must put life before love.'

'Then get me to my ship with haste,' Michael demanded. 'There may still be a chance. If Louise is the woman I think her, she will delay that wedding in any way she can.'

Peter tried to smile, tried to catch the hope that lit Michael's eyes.

'Luke and Denzil can manage that task, Michael. There's something I must do before I leave France.'

Michael nodded, understanding at once. 'André?' he said.

'Aye, I must bury his body before I go. He's lain in that field too long already, but I dare not do it before. I'll join you on the boat when I've seen him safe in a grave and said a prayer over him.'

SEVENTEEN

The bank was laced with lady smock, a multitude of tiny flowers tinted with the palest pink and lilac. A kingfisher rose suddenly, a flash of dazzling blue and green, from amongst the grasses; startled no doubt by the rattling of the carriage wheels and the deep thud of horses' hooves on hard, dried mud. There were marsh marigolds now, rich in gold, scattered over a meadow that stretched right down to the water. Deep footprints in the sodden earth there, showed where the cows had trundled their way to drink. Slowly, they lifted their heads, chewing, watching unconcerned as another carriage made its jolting way towards Dartmouth church.

Louise stared unseeing from the carriage window. She did not notice the heron that stood so patiently at the water's edge, awaiting its next meal. She did not know that as the carriage turned away from the river and rumbled beneath budding hedgerows, there were snowdrops still hiding beneath them and the deep purple of the violet already in flower to take their place. Today was her wedding day, a day she had done everything in her limited power to prevent. Today she rode, completely defeated, beside Sir Joshua, who was to give her in marriage to his only son in the village church.

Neither the choosing of flowers nor the buying of a trousseau had brought enthusiasm into Louise's aching heart. She had performed whatever was necessary in a dream, knowing that the one person who might have saved her from this miserable fate was, it was assumed, dead. There was no longer any purpose in her life, save doing her duty and marrying the man whom her imprisoned father had said she must marry. When the news of Peter's death reached her she had said nothing. When George had told her that he himself had managed to get a message through to her father, she had believed him without question, never doubting it to be the truth. Why Peter could not have done what had seemed to be so simple for George, she had not considered. The time, the month was past and had Peter been successful in his dangerous mission then he would have undoubtedly returned long ago. Peter was dead, like André he had died for her, and she must expect no happiness in life for herself now.

The dress she wore was of heavy cream silk, embroidered with tiny rosebuds of the palest pink. Her bouquet, too, was of rosebuds, fresh from the gardens of Rutherford Hall, their delicate pink petals just awakening to the spring. The horses pulled more slowly now, descending between closely wooded copses. The mass of trees was broken only by the odd cart track or footpath.

'By Gad, I wish you were a little more enthusiastic Louise!' Sir Joshua exclaimed, peering into her face through his monocle. 'It would seem you consider it your funeral instead of your wedding day.'

Louise made an effort to smile. He had after all been very kind to her since her arrival from Cornwall. She should be grateful to him at least for her gowns and jewellery.

'I am perhaps a little afraid,' she offered meekly. 'It is the first time that I have been married.'

The attempt at a mild joke brought a

broad smile to her companion's face. 'Not a bad fellow, George, you know. Nothing to be afraid of. Thinks a deuce of a lot of you, too. Quite surprising, considering...' He stopped abruptly, realising that that line of conversation was hardly appropriate for his son's future wife. 'I expect you are looking forward to London. Wants to show you off, what! Don't blame him either. Did just the same with his mother.' He sighed. 'Remind me of her like the blazes you do. Did I tell you that? Well, yes, I suppose I did. Lovely girl she was. Twist me round her little finger, by Gad. You take me word. You'll have George dancing attention on you, if you play your cards right.' He laughed, straightening his wig which had become slightly awry on the seat on the coach. 'Don't need to tell you that, I'll wager. You're a woman. Women always know how to get what they want.'

He went on rambling, but Louise hardly heard him. She had no wish to twist George Rutherford around her finger. She simply did not want him at all. The coach lurched quite suddenly. Then the horses whinnied and came abruptly to a halt. Sir Joshua pulled down the window to see what was amiss. Thrusting out his head to shout up at the coachman.

'By Gad!' he exclaimed, his face white as his powdered wig. 'It's a highwayman! We're being held up! And I with not a weapon in sight.' He thrust out his head and shouted across to the offending horseman. 'See here, my man. There's a bride in here on her way to her wedding. Wouldn't want to spoil her wedding day. What! Now, let us go on, my good fellow. We'll be late at the altar.'

They heard a laugh; the man rode along beside the coach his pistol aimed directly at Sir Joshua's protruding head.

'Then I will take a look at the maid, my good sir. If you would be as good as to step down and assist the lady to the ground.'

Sir Joshua scowled. For a moment he was about to object, but the pistol moved slightly closer, so he pulled back his head and undid the door catch.

Louise felt surprisingly calm. Indeed this sudden diversion from the fate ahead of her struck her as decidedly funny. When she should have been trembling in her shoes she was needing great self-will to stifle a giggle. The man on the horse was dressed completely in black. A long, black cloak fell easily from his shoulders and draped behind him over the horse's back. Under his black tricorne, he wore a curled wig and concealing part of his face was a black silk mask. His voice was not unpleasant although he spoke with an accent which Sir Joshua noted with annoyance.

'Cornishman, damned Cornishman!' he muttered under his breath as he stepped down onto the lane and proceeded to hand down Louise with less than his usual grace.

'My apologies, Mistress,' the horseman said, sweeping off his hat and bowing his head towards her. 'Some man is indeed fortunate to be awaiting such a beautiful bride.' For a moment he seemed to hesitate, then he replaced his hat and turned his eyes back to Sir Joshua. 'Your purse, Sir, would hasten your departure, and a gold watch and chain I'll wager. Pray hand them to me slowly.' He glanced at the coachman still cringing on the box. 'Down here by your master!' he commanded, 'and no idle trickery or there'll be a ball straight through his heart.'

The frightened man climbed down hastily and sidled up to Sir Joshua who was busy disengaging the timepiece. Bringing his horse nearer, the highwayman held out an ungloved hand. 'And your snuff box, Sir?' he added as if an afterthought. This was produced reluctantly, then the horse moved forward and halted by Louise. She lifted her eyes to the black mask, wondering what sort of man it was beneath this disguise.

' 'Twill be a pity to spoil your wedding finery, Mistress, but I fancy that necklace would fetch a fair price. I'll wager your husband will not miss it.'

She unclasped the sapphire and let it trickle into his waiting hand. For a brief second she stared incredulously at his fingers then she raised her eyes to his smiling face. Quickly he slipped the necklace into his pocket, then touching the horse's belly gently with his boot, he moved back a little into the cart track from where he had first appeared.

'Back onto your box, my man,' he shouted to the coachman. 'And make haste for the lady is late.'

The coachman scrambled hurriedly up and grasped the reins in readiness...

'Now you, Sir. Pray open the door for the lady.'

Sir Joshua turned to the door, his face dark with anger and humiliation. In the same instant the horse came forward its rider bent low, grasped a surprised Louise around the waist and lifted her easily up onto the saddle in front of him, reasserting the aim of his pistol as he did so.

'Pray keep still, Sir,' he warned as Sir Joshua made as if to cross to the horse. ' 'Tis a fancy I have to take the lady to her wedding myself. She'll come to no harm, you've my word on that.'

'The word of a highwayman and a thief?'

'An honourable one, Sir. I'll say it again. No harm will come to the lady. I shall see she is at the church in good time for her wedding.' He turned his horse, thrust the pistol into his belt, then rode off hard down the cart track with one arm tight around Louise's slim waist.

She had not screamed or even struggled when he had lifted her up onto his horse. Perchance she thought it a better fate to be abducted by a strange highwayman than to be wed to George Rutherford.

'I am amazed you have not tried to unmask me,' he told her good humouredly. ' 'Twould be easy enough from where you are.'

'Do I need to take off a mask to know

a man I love,' she whispered.

He laughed, took off the black silk mask himself and tossed it into the hedge. 'Am I so bad at disguise?' he enquired, 'that you knew me at once, Cornish accent and all.'

She smiled. 'Not at once, Peter, but you wear my ring, and when I looked up into your eyes they were so bright and blue.' She sighed. 'Can this really be true? Tell me that I am not dreaming. Will I wake in a coach and find myself led to the altar?'

He slowed the horse and turned her to face him. 'Indeed you will, my darling, but 'twill be your father beside you and me that you will meet at the altar.'

She gasped, amazed. 'My father!'

'Aye, he's at Camelford by now. Not well, I fear, but I've a notion he'll recover with good food and care.'

'And will he allow me to marry you?' she asked eagerly.

Peter laughed, took off the wig and tossed it away. 'I've his word on it, and a man of the Church to witness it.' He kissed her gently, then kicked the horse into action again. 'A mile or two and there's a good inn I know. You'll find a change of clothes, and a carriage,

I hope, to take us home.' He grinned suddenly. 'I would I could see George Rutherford's face; jilted at the altar, he'll die of humiliation.'

She leaned her head on his chest and sighed. 'Maman will be so very angry with me.' Then suddenly she lifted her head, gave a whoop of delight, took out the pins which held her veil firm and taking it off, she tossed the whole headdress and her bouquet into the plough-ribbed field.

Peter laughed, still hardly believing that he had reached her in time. Then he reined in the horse before springing down to the ground and lifting her down beside him. He walked away from her for a moment, bending down among the wayside grasses. When he turned back to her he held out a small bouquet of flowers. Violets, snowdrops and lady smock. 'Like you,' he whispered. 'Unbelievably beautiful, and unbelievably mine...'

Michael Pendeen returned swiftly to the stables and threw a saddle onto a fresh horse. The air was warm as he rode away from his house; the tall chestnuts and sprawling oaks were bright with new leaves, their flowers tight in bud, waiting for May

313

Time. The hedgerows, too, echoed the coming of spring, and the brown ribbed fields made patchwork with the green squares of the hay fields.

Michael left the copse and turned his horse into a narrow, winding lane, heading westwards towards the coast. His arm, held firm in a sling, under his coat was painful and he had longed for rest and a warm bed. Seigneur de Chauvelin had both of those now and the Doctor had been sent for, but someone had been absent from Michael's home when he had ridden there so exhausted. He followed the fresh hoofprints now, searching for the strength to make just one more short journey before he rested.

Soon, he came upon one of his own horses, tethered fast by its reins to the stones on the hedge a short way from the cliff. He dismounted quickly and left his horse tied in the same way. When he crossed the cliff top turf, he climbed with surprisingly agility up the last rocky slope, until in the distance he saw a woman standing alone at the edge of the cliff, gazing out over the hazy blue of the sea.

Weariness left him as he strode with a bursting heart towards her. He shouted loudly when he thought she might hear him, but the wind blew it back to him and her head did not turn. 'Rosalie!' he called again and this time she heard her name and swung round to face him, her cloak blown out in the wind.

When she saw him she did not move, she stood motionless, staring as if she did not believe it was he.

'Aye, 'tis I. 'Tis no apparition you see, my love,' he shouted. And then she laughed, and ran, tears flowing freely down her cheeks until he kissed them away.

'I lost the baby,' she whispered suddenly, and he nodded and held her close.

'Aye, I know. Alice told me. And I was not here.'

'You are here now,' she said, then the tears flowed again. 'Our son has a birthday tomorrow, and you're here for that!' She stood back from him and looked up into his face. 'I thought you dead, Michael. I truly thought you dead.'

'I don't die that easy, Rosalie. You should know it well enough. And did not the Lord make a promise. "I will be with thee. I will not fail thee or forsake thee." He kept that promise, my love, and I've felt him close though the times were hard.'

'And the baby, Michael. Was the Lord with me when I lost the child?' she said bitterly.

He nodded slowly. 'Aye, 'tis certain he was. My mother always says that nature deals best with her own. 'Tis likely the child was malformed in mind or body.' He smiled. 'We've time enough now to make another, a dozen if you like.'

She laughed and blushed as he had meant her to. Then she saw his coat and the sleeve that hung limply by his side. 'You're hurt, Michael!' she exclaimed with dismay.

He grinned, he had quite forgotten about the pain, but now it came back to him with a rush. 'Only a scratch from a knife. 'Twill be well enough with a little care from you and a clean cloth on it. You have not asked about Peter, or even Seigneur de Chauvelin?' he chided her gently.

'Then tell me,' she begged, 'for I have cursed Peter a thousand times for taking you away from me. Was it worth it, this voyage? Did you find this man?'

'Aye, we brought him here, he was near to death in more ways than one. But we got him safe and he gave his word that Peter shall have Louise. We kept North along the Channel and took Peter into Dartmouth on our way. 'Tis likely he'll bring Louise to Camelford at once to see her father.'

Rosalie laughed, pushed back the long hair that was blowing around her face, then they began walking back towards their horses, his one good arm held firm around her shoulders.

'And if Ben ever thinks he fancies a French wife, Michael Pendeen,' she warned him. 'Then you will lock him up in the pillory.'

He laughed down at her and bent to whisper in her ear: 'There's always Marrietta,' he reminded her. 'Another four years and I doubt he will think her quite so terrible.'

She was smiling now, her face alive with happiness. He thought suddenly of André, but as he watched her, he would not spoil the moment of joy. There would be time enough for him to share his own sadness for the man who had not escaped from Châteaunoir.

The publishers hope that this book has given you enjoyable reading. Large Print Books are especially designed to be as easy to see and hold as possible. If you wish a complete list of our books, please ask at your local library or write directly to: Dales Large Print Books, Long Preston, North Yorkshire, BD23 4ND, England.